Berzerker

J.M. DABNEY

ISBN-10: 1-947184-02-4
ISBN-13: 978-1-947184-02-2

DEDICATION

To the lovers of all characters no matter size or shape, color, religion or lack thereof. Because as it should be Love is Love.

AUTHOR'S NOTE

Although this is a series each title can be read as a standalone with a Happily Ever After and no Cliffhanger.

Thank you for Reading!

CONTENTS

1 BLACK LEATHER, A HAIRY BELLY AND KNUCKLE TATTOOS

Today proved he shouldn't have fucking bothered getting out of bed. Brian sat at his station in Twirled World Ink and tried not to sink into the floor with the need to disappear. Was it only twenty-four hours earlier he'd fooled himself into believing he could have something good? He scrubbed his huge, tattooed hands over his face and ruffled his thick beard. If he cared, he'd think it was time for a trim, but he didn't. Before the ex, he was happy with who he was.

For a year and a half, he'd dated the same guy, which was a record for him. Before it was a few months tops and then he'd find some excuse to run. With his attitude and gruff nature, the only place he fit was with the other crazies of Twirled. Finding someone for a quick blow job or fuck was easy enough, but contrary to outward appearance, he wanted weird things—a relationship with a guy that saw him beyond the tattoos, belly and his *Harley Fatboy*— someone who took the time to look past all the shit everyone considered flaws.

A rumble sounded in his chest, and he shook his head.

Ron was a bit out of his league. He'd always assumed the slick, pretty man was slumming or whatever. When they'd moved in together a year ago, he pushed his insecurities aside. The rational part of his brain told his ass not to move in, but did he listen: fuck no.

A few months ago, Ron received a promotion at work, started looking for houses and eventually, he'd found the perfect one. It was too flashy for Brian's tastes, but he thought he'd get used to it. It turns out he didn't have to worry about that. Ron never intended him to live there.

Which was the reason he was at work on his day off, hours ahead of the doors opening. He was homeless, and it wasn't the first time. Well, maybe he wasn't homeless. He could definitely go back to the Twirled House. Most of his friends lived in the same place, and he knew no one rented out his old room, yet he couldn't make himself call Trouble and explain what was going on.

Trouble and the rest never liked Ron, understandable since Ron wasn't exactly the bike runs and roadhouse type. They worked long, weird hours so when they had free time they partied hard and hung out. Ron thought it unnecessary to spend so much time with the people you worked and lived with.

The fateful and soon-to-be-realized fucked up day he met the man was when Ron came in to get his first ink done. A maze of scroll work with initials hidden within its depths. It looked like something you'd find on a wrought iron gate in front of a stuffy old mansion. That should've been his first damn clue.

He hadn't been a fan of it, but really, it was Ron's skin. He could do what he wanted with it. A few weeks later they'd went on a date. If he looked back with an objective mind, then he'd have realized earlier it was a disaster in the making. He just couldn't put his finger on the early signs.

"Zerk?"

A beautiful masculine voice jerked his attention to the back of the shop when Landon Phelps his boss' son appeared, a huge smile on his too gorgeous face. He shouldn't be noticing anything on Landon was gorgeous or otherwise.

"Can't stay away from the place, not even on your day off," Landon quipped.

"Hey, Landon, what you doing here?"

He didn't want to go into details about why he was there. Landon was a sweet guy, but he was also best friends with the rest of the shop Crew. They'd know all the bullshit in no time. Fuckers were famous for group texts.

"Berzerker."

Oh fuck, he knew that tone, and in no more than three syllables, the man brought him to his proverbial knees ready to confess. Landon was like a feeling's barometer. No one kept secrets from him. Someone could utter one word, and Landon was all over their mood. He'd never met someone as empathetic as Landon. It was annoying sometimes, especially when things were best kept to oneself.

A Twirled intervention was not on his to-do list anytime soon.

"What?" He was about to get up when a compact soft body sat sideways on his lap. "Personal space, Landon." He knew it was pointless as soon as the statement was out of his mouth.

"You've worked here three years, when have I cared about your personal space?"

He knew he wasn't getting out of it, so he just blurted out his latest fuck up. "Ron broke up with me."

"And? He was a bit of a douche." Landon paused and then turned a questioning look to him. "Wait, weren't you two supposed to move into your new place today?"

"His new place, he never intended for me to go with him. He packed his shit and left mine behind." He cleared his throat and started to perfectly imitate Ron, "I have a look and reputation to protect now and an ugly man like you—"

"Fuck him."

The sheer vehemence in Landon's tone took him by surprise.

No matter growing up in a rough bike and tattoo world, Landon rarely cursed until he had a few drinks in him. The last time they got him drunk, they'd counted the times Landon said the word fuck, but they'd lost track halfway through the night. He was also a drunk cuddler, and Zerk would admit it was cute when Landon did it.

"So, we moving you home?"

Landon asked as if it was a foregone conclusion. Since he'd taken the job at Twirled, there'd been a steady revolving door until recently. They'd finally solidified a Crew in the last year.

"I don't think I can deal with the I-told-you-so right now." He loved the guys, but they could be assholes when proved right.

"That's just everyone being them."

"I can stay in a motel for a few days until—"

"Not a damn chance. This is what's happening...you can come home with me."

"I can't do—"

He almost started laughing at the constant interruptions. It was classic Landon. If he wasn't getting his way, he'd hammer away by cutting someone off until they conceded victory to him.

"Of course you can."

"Quit interrupting—"

"No. Look. I'm rarely there with my work schedule and traveling. You can lick your wounds and get over the butt hurt. Although, I know you like the butt—"

He couldn't resist the laughter that started deep in his chest. "Can I say for all the preppy khaki cuteness, you're an asshole."

"See you and assholes," Landon looked so smug. "Come on. Let me get the paperwork so I can do the books tonight and we'll go home."

"I can't—"

"You can, or I'll force you to look at the pictures the parental units sent me."

"No," Zerk shouted.

Gib and Peaches were off on their yearly anniversary getaway, and this year it was some nudist resort in the Caribbean. He didn't think Landon had pictures with naked body parts, but he sure as fuck didn't want to chance it.

Zerk still had to look down at Landon even with the man on his lap and watched an onyx brow slowly lift.

"Fine, but it's only until I find another place." He agreed as his gut told him he would.

"Deal, but it's not like I don't have the room for you and Herc. Speaking of Herc, where's my boy?"

"He's chilling in the moving van. I was just trying to figure out what the fuck I was going to do."

"You left him alone. You know how sensitive the baby is," Landon shouted.

He nearly fell before Zerk caught him and settled him securely on his lap.

"Well, we got a plan. I'll grab everything, and you can follow me home. We can get you moved in and settled, but then I have to go to the office for a bit."

"Okay." He agreed because he didn't see any other option. More than likely he'd be back living with his friends soon, but he needed some time to himself.

❧ ❧ ❧

A few hours later, Zerk stood in a sparsely decorated guest room. Just a queen-size bed, a dresser and functional nightstands. Landon left a few minutes before to head back to the office.

To be honest, he figured he should be devastated, but he was more dinged up by Ron's parting shots about his looks and job. He'd grown up on a ranch in East Texas. He was as at home on horseback as he was his *Harley Fatboy*. The soft hum of his tattoo machine soothed him as nothing else in his life ever had.

The sketches he'd started as a child turned into a dream when one of his father's new hands hired on. Stu had been covered in colorful ink, and at eight, he'd asked the man so many questions. He'd started his apprenticeship as soon as he'd battled his dad for freedom. Zerk loved the ranch, but there was something about those tattoos and the stories that went along with them. They had drawn him more than the sun rising on the land he'd assumed would be his one day.

He hadn't looked back or regretted it for one second, regrets weren't in his makeup.

A heavy weight settled against his leg, and he looked down at Herc. The English mastiff topped out at a solid two hundred pounds. The original owner hadn't realized the care involved in having such a large pet. Zerk's sheer size of six-five and two hundred and seventy pounds made Herc perfect for him.

A loud huff made him shake his head. "He'll be home soon. Just don't get too attached; we won't be here long."

Telling Herc not to get attached to his already favorite person was stupid. The massive dog didn't pay attention to anyone except Zerk. Although once he'd started working for Twirled and Landon walked through the door the first time, Herc was attached to the man's hip any time he was around.

"Let's get unpacked and settled in. Landon'll be home at six, maybe we can throw together something for dinner."

Another loud harrumph and he was left alone. Great. His dog was going to sulk. Not only did he lose his boyfriend, but his dog had a new favorite. "Pathetic, Anderson, that's what you are. Pathetic."

2 THE MISSION IS A GO

His man, his man, was in his house and that's where Zerk was staying. Landon waited too damn long for Brian "Berzerker" Anderson to get rid of that douche boyfriend. If he could just get past his insecurities, jump Zerk and claim all that sexy burly man, then he'd be happy. Well, not jump him exactly, but that was on the to-do list too. He just didn't know if he could do it. Fantasy and reality were two entirely different things, and real Zerk liked him as a friend, while fantasy Zerk never left Landon's bed.

He'd known he was different from his peers and even in his own family since he realized he never quite fit. Landon grew up in one tattoo shop or another since he could remember. At first, he learned the business at his mother or father's knees. His lullaby was the hum of a tattoo machine as it moved over virgin skin. Bikers and freaks were his babysitters. Although sweet, short and slim, Landon was always on the outside looking in at his family and friends.

He was a stuffy accountant with no tattoos to his name. He'd decided to get one and then the day he was going to schedule it, Zerk showed up at Twirled. Landon had decided it wasn't the right time yet, but deep down he'd known the truth. No one else would do the ink. The sketch was tacked up over Zerk's station and had been for three years. Every time Zerk asked him was he ready, all Landon could say was not yet.

Zerk didn't understand what the tattoo meant. Not the design, but that held significance too, but it was Landon's claim on the big, gruff man. To him, there was an intimacy to the art, an undeniable trust. Needles piercing skin and inking permanence into a blank canvas. He trusted Zerk, but Landon didn't trust himself—just yet.

Ordering Zerk to move in with him was the first step. So far that was the only step, but he'd figure out the rest of the *Win Zerk Mission* later.

He gathered his laptop bag from the passenger seat and opened his door, slipping from the car. For a few minutes, he longingly stared at his garage where his vintage Knucklehead languished. He needed to take the guys up on one of their Sunday runs soon. It had been months since he'd been out with them.

Not wanting to wait any longer, he jogged toward the front door and opened it. Walking inside, he called out to Zerk. "Honey, I'm home."

Huge paws on hardwood greeted him seconds before Herc was barreling toward him. "Hi, baby." He sat his bag aside and knelt on the floor to give Herc scratches. The fearsome animal whined like a big baby.

"He's either been in your bed or beside the door all damn day." Zerk grumped, and Landon couldn't help laughing at the man's sulk.

Zerk leaned against the door frame pouting and rolling his eyes, but it was the strip of hairy belly that nearly made him drool before he controlled himself. In all the years he'd known Zerk, never once had he seen the man shirtless. That little peek of the rounded belly was the most erotic thing he'd ever seen. Man, he was sad, he laughed to himself.

"He missed me. You rescinded visitation when you got with the douche."

"Yeah, yeah, I made that chicken stir fry you like for dinner."

"Great, thanks," With one last rub, Landon pushed to his feet. "Let me get changed and I'll be right back."

"No hurry. The rice has a few more minutes."

Landon nodded and headed for his room.

Okay, he needed clothes. His whole nudist lifestyle had to change. He'd grown up in a house and family where nudity was normal. He didn't have the greatest body, but he wasn't ashamed of it. Not everyone could look like some cut supermodel, and he wasn't attracted to the slick, perfect look either. Gruff and husky Zerk was just his type, especially that hairy belly and thick, grab worthy beard.

He changed quickly into a pair of loose, seen better days' jeans and a t-shirt that didn't quite meet the waistband leaving his flat stomach exposed. Landon mussed his perfectly styled hair leaving it in a mess of uncontrolled waves. For work, he parted it to the side and tamed it with unknown amounts of product to put on a façade of professionalism. At home, he preferred the sex-mussed bed-head look. Sadly, it only got that way by him using his fingers to mess it up.

He didn't want to think about how long it had been since he'd been fucked—or even had someone fuck him how he liked to be fucked. The last guy he'd dated for a few months was way too gentle. Landon sighed, he couldn't remember the last time a man left him with fingertip bruises on his hips or bite marks—bruises his shirt would tease all day and remind him of the night or morning before. He might be tiny by male standards, but dammit, he wanted to be manhandled. Sex bruises were the best bruises.

The scents of dinner called his name. He hadn't taken the time to grab lunch since he'd brought Zerk back to his house to get settled. He walked down the hall, and he entered the kitchen to find the massive man with his back to him. Landon smirked and headed straight for him. He wrapped his arms around Zerk's waist. "I'm keeping you," he stated as he leaned to the side to see around Zerk's mass.

"Don't get used to it. You know my weird hours."

"I'm still on those weird hours. Too many years of being at the shop and time zone differences with work trips. What do you need help with?"

"Nothing, the table's already set. Just need to make the plates."

"Let me grab them, and we can eat," He stepped away to grab plates, "Plans tonight? Trouble sent me a text earlier about everyone getting together about ten at Scary's for beer and billiards."

"His house or the bar?"

"Bar. He complained of cleanup and all the bodies he had to step over the next morning. I think the last straw was when he found Trouble naked in the middle of his living room and had no idea how he got that way."

"Trouble doesn't need a reason to get that way."

Trouble was a sweetheart. He became friends with him when they were kids, and until Trouble went off to a short-lived run at college, they'd been inseparable. His best friend had some shit going on, but it wasn't his place to share Trouble's secrets, not even with Zerk.

"I didn't want to tell him I took his clothes."

"Why the fuck did you take his clothes?"

"He lost them in a bet."

"Why would—" Zerk shook his head and turned his attention back to the stove. "I don't even want to know."

"You definitely don't."

It wasn't that bad of a story or even much of a secret.

"No, now I'm curious."

"Okay, but if you tell Trouble, he'll kill me."

"Oh, this has to be bad."

"No," He handed plates to Zerk. "He keeps getting turned down by this guy he's interested in."

"No one turns him down."

Zerk dished up the food, and Landon took the plates to the table.

"Beer," Zerk asked.

"Thanks." Landon set the plates down on the table and took a seat. "Trouble's been asking him out for months and gets turned down every time. He's in a full-on pout. So, he was feeling cocky with a few extra beers in him, and I told him he didn't have a chance with the cutie. He said hundredth time would be the charm. It wasn't, so he's been avoiding him since. It didn't help that he had me as an audience to his mortification."

"I'm sure. He's model perfect with a touch of bad boy that men love, and he never has a problem getting a date or just taking someone home for the night."

"I think it's good for him. He's become spoiled." Life wasn't as easy for Trouble as people assumed, but again, it wasn't his place to share.

"Yes, he has."

"This is amazing." Landon sighed as he stared at his plate.

They settled in to eat and lapsed into a comfortable silence. He couldn't help sneaking glances across the small table.

He'd known Zerk for years, and that was the first time they were ever alone. Someone was always around, or it was just them in the shop, but never like this. So close he could touch Zerk without interruption, yet the time for touching hadn't come. But fuck he wanted to. He could picture it, getting up from his chair and moving slowly around the table to place himself in Zerk's lap. Finally get that kiss he'd fantasized about since he'd met the big man.

If he was anything, he was patient A little more time, and Zerk would be his—he just needed to wait until the time was right. That is, if he didn't die of frustration first because Zerk never gave him the impression he saw him as anything but a friend or the boss' son.

3 THE CREW DOES FEW THINGS WELL AND ONE OF THEM IS GIVE HIM SHIT

His pardon only lasted until Zerk finished with his first client of the day. That was when the crew smelled blood in the water like sharks at a fucking feeding frenzy.

"What's this we hear about you living with Landon," Trouble asked, amused.

He groaned as his four friends lined up with their arms crossed on the half wall and rested chins on their forearms. Trouble, Scary, Priest and Lucky batted their lashes at him, except Scary who just glared at him. For some reason, Scary was super protective of Landon. He figured that was because the rough man started working for Gib and Peaches a decade ago as one of the first artists at Twirled.

"Ron—"

"Figured he'd stop slumming and move on to bigger and better things." Scary didn't even pose it as a question.

"Yeah, thanks, I needed that."

"You're welcome."

"Why didn't you come back to Twirled House? We never rented out your room. Hell, we're the only ones that can put up with each other." Trouble stared at him until he felt the need to shift.

"He thought we'd give him shit about the prick kicking him to the curb and finding a prettier man." Lucky was as eloquent as always. Lucky was affectionately known as the hyper hippie. With his childhood of radical honesty, it was a surprise Lucky was as well-adjusted as he appeared. Which didn't exactly say much for Lucky's stability. Everyone wanted to kill him within the first five minutes.

"He didn't find a prettier man, or at least I don't think—" Now wasn't that depressing. Was it possible that he wasn't just dumped, but cheated on also? Fucking great, like his pride needed another direct hit.

"How do you know," Lucky asked.

"You're just a fucking ray of sunshine."

"I try. So why don't you come back?"

"I just need some space to think. It's not a big deal. Landon's not home much because of work, so I've got plenty of space."

"Y'all know he's always had a thing for pretty little Landon right," Lucky spoke up.

Zerk could've knocked the mouthy bastard out. "Man, keep your bullshit to yourself. You really have to learn some things don't need to be said."

"I grew up with a house that preferred radical honesty as a parenting method. Why lie about something when the truth might get you just what you fucking want? In this case, the pretty man bent over the nearest surface in your new shared living space."

Trouble smacked the back of Lucky's head. "Ignore him, I can't believe you picked living with Landon. We're family, man, yeah we'd give ya shit, but you know that's just our way."

"I know, but—"

"No buts, he wants some alone time with Landon." Lucky was fucking asking for it.

"I don't want alone time with Landon. He's my friend like he is with the rest of y'all."

They all snorted and started to wander away. He knew it wasn't the end. His crew was just in regrouping mode, and they'd strike when he least expected it.

It wasn't like he didn't notice Landon was an extremely attractive man. Ron was handsome, but Landon was downright gorgeous and completely out of Zerk's league. Okay, to be honest, Landon never made him feel less than. He was a cuddler and someone who was naturally affectionate. He never hesitated to give someone a hug. Hell, his favorite seat was Zerk's lap. No one ever seemed to find it strange.

He remembered the day he met Landon. It was a week after he was hired and it was his first day, Zerk nearly shit himself when he got the call that he was joining Twirled. Gib Phelps was a legend, studied under some of the greatest artists to ever hit the scene. Zerk felt like he'd finally made it. Gib and Scary met him the first afternoon, set him up with a station and that's when Peaches walked in with Landon.

He had this thick wavy hair perfectly styled. Although he'd worn faded jeans and a plain white V-neck t-shirt that showed off smooth pale skin, he looked elegant as fuck. The next thing he'd noticed was the virgin skin. There wasn't any ink or piercing in sight. Freckles dusted his flesh. Zerk's hands had itched to touch each tiny mark. Then Gib introduced him and immediately Landon Phelps was off limits.

He spun his chair and looked up at the beautiful drawing framed next to the mirror. It would be Landon's first tattoo. He'd given Zerk the drawing not long after he started and by silent agreement, no one but Zerk would do it. He was amazed by Landon's talent although he shouldn't have been surprised.

It was an abstract, images intermingled to form bodies, a couple in an intimate position, but who they were was unknown. He was sure one was Landon. Something about it was erotic in its innocent appearance. At first glance, it was inkblots, like a Rorschach Test, yet, more refined. He asked at least every couple of weeks if Landon was ready and Landon would look at him with a small smile then just say: not yet.

A primitive need to mark his perfect body overwhelmed him. It seemed from the day Landon gave him the drawing, it grew and built with a burning intensity.

"Still not letting you ink him?" Trouble's voice came from behind him.

"Nope, he doesn't seem ready yet."

"I don't think you'll have to wait much longer."

"What do you mean," Zerk asked and spun back around.

"You're free of Ron. I've known Landon forever. We went to school together. He got tons of shit because of his family and friends. Landon is extremely selective when it comes to partners. When he walked into Twirled the day you started, I thought he was going to swallow his tongue. You're exactly his type."

"I doubt that."

"I don't. That future tattoo right there…" Trouble pointed to the frame. "Is his claim. The first true act of intimacy. You may not think so, but the moment that graces his skin you're his."

"You're full of shit."

"Think what you want, big man, but Landon wants you. If you weren't so fucked up in the head by shit relationships, you might have seen it earlier."

"There can't be anything. Gib would lose his shit."

"Nope, Gib lets Landon run his own life, always has. Unusual upbringing. Landon announced he was gay when he was five. A girl cousin said she was going to marry Prince Charming one day, he said he was too. Gib and Peaches went with the flow."

"Gib and Peaches are cool as fuck though."

"Yes, they are, and if you made a play for Landon, it wouldn't even cause a ripple."

"Landon's gorgeous though. I mean everyone looks like a troll compared to him."

"You're biased."

"Fuck I am, Landon goes out with guys all the time."

"When's the last time you saw him dating anyone?"

"I don't know, he was seeing that guy from his office, I think."

"No, that ended after a few dates. Landon invited him on one of our runs. You were out of town visiting your folks. You should've seen the guys face when he pulled up to see all of us. When Landon told him to hop on the back of his bike, you would've thought Landon asked him to jump into a pit of vipers. He left the man standing beside his Mercedes and roared away with the rest of us.

"Landon's professional life isn't going to ever mesh with his personal one. Just because he doesn't look like one of us, he still is and existing in the void between them is killing his spirit. Take a chance, Zerk. Everyone knows you want Landon and he wants you. You just have to get over this bullshit in your head." Trouble smacked his shoulder and headed to his own station to get ready for an appointment.

Zerk shook his head and wondered if Trouble was right. Landon did take the opportunity to take a seat on his lap before he did it with anyone else.

Ron came by the shop one day to find them all sitting around, Landon leaning back against his chest. Landon instantly vacated to allow Ron to take his place, but the man snarled his nose. Had Ron ever touched him just because outside the bedroom? Even in the beginning of their relationship, Ron had frowned on Zerk touching him. Hell, he tried to bend Ron over the kitchen table one day, and everything went to hell after that.

His high sex drive turned into a major point of contention between them, also his fetish for marking his partners. The very few bite marks and bruises Zerk left had earned him disgust and nights on the couch. Fuck, he was pathetic, he should have known Ron and him were going nowhere. He dropped his head back and heavily sighed.

"Epiphany?"

"Shut up. Gloating isn't attractive." He growled, but it only made Trouble cackle and look smugger than he normally did.

"Gloating is appropriate when I'm right."

Zerk surged from his chair and left to get some coffee with Trouble's laughter following him. "You're an asshole," he yelled as the door closed behind him. He looked through the front window to find Trouble making kissy faces at him. Zerk couldn't wait for that bastard to get his due and hoped it was as embarrassing and uncomfortable as he felt right then.

4 ATTACK OF THE NUDIST

Landon slapped at his alarm, screaming for it to die. He wasn't a morning person by any stretch of the imagination. Rolling out of bed with his eyes still closed, he padded barefoot out of his bedroom toward the kitchen. He still couldn't make himself sleep at night which made his boring, respectable nine-to-five hell on most days.

The scent of strong coffee teased his senses as soon as he walked into the room. One eye popped open as he looked around his kitchen. Zerk's helmet and backpack were on the table, his huge boots turned over next to the door that led to the garage. He started the music app on his phone and poured himself an oversized mug. He spun to lean against the counter and crossed his ankles, rubbed his hand over his flat stomach and chest.

He moaned with pleasure at the first sip. It was a sad day in his life when he even thought coffee was better than sex. Oh shit, no thinking about sex with Zerk in the house.

Only two weeks had passed since Zerk took up residence in his house, and he barely resisted the urge to touch Zerk all the time. It wasn't as if he didn't touch Zerk a lot. He was always a touchy-feely guy; his parents were affectionate, and it had passed on to him. Except he didn't want to touch Zerk like he did Trouble or Lucky or any of the other guys.

Most of the time he wanted to curl up in Zerk's lap anywhere and everywhere. Tempering his need was becoming a full-time job.

"Fuck," Zerk's voice boomed through the house.

He shot his gaze to the door to find Zerk's back to him and then down at himself—he'd forgotten clothes.

"Oh shit, I'm sorry." He reached for a dish towel and held it in front of himself. Great, thinking about Zerk's lap had caused his dick to harden. It is fucking embarrassing.

"What's going on? Did you bring someone—"

"No, I didn't bring anyone home. Normally I don't wear clothes around the house, and this is the first time I've forgotten since you've been here. I'm covered sort of, you can turn around."

"Are you sure?"

Landon almost laughed at the question but knew it wouldn't be appropriate. "Yes."

Zerk hesitantly glanced over his massive shoulder, and the man's eyes widened.

"What are you doing up so early?"

"Couldn't sleep."

"Well, the coffee's fresh. I'm going to go get ready for work. I really am sorry," Landon wasn't sorry at all.

The big man's eyes slowly moved over his body, and he couldn't mistake the appreciation or heat in his gaze. He walked toward the door, and Zerk turned to the side to make room for him to pass, but Landon stopped and faced him. "I'm ready."

"Ready, ready for what?"

"The tattoo." That's all Landon said before he continued from the kitchen and toward his bedroom. He felt lighter than he had in the year and a half since Zerk started dating Ron. The man was his, and it was time he claimed him. His hatred of mornings disappeared as he smiled and started making plans. Zerk would be in his bed soon.

✦✦✦

Dammit. His day started off amazingly, and now it all went to shit. He loved his job as a forensic accountant and worked hard to earn the place and respect he'd received over the past three years. The only thing about his job he didn't like was the traveling. For the next two weeks, he'd be trapped in some office going over a decade's worth of accounts to find out where the owner was hiding money. In his opinion, it already hit a non-extradition country, and Mr. Embezzler would disappear into the night.

He had to go home and tell Zerk he'd be out of town. Landon pulled into his garage surprised to see Zerk's *Fatboy* parked next to his Knucklehead, Zerk was never home that early. He turned off the engine and quickly gathered his things, and then headed inside.

When he walked into the kitchen, he found Zerk leaned back against the counter having a staring contest with Herc.

"What did our son do now?"

"He hid my keys and wallet. They were on my bed when I went to take a shower, now they're gone."

"Why do you think he did it? He's such a good boy." Landon laughed as Herc trotted over to him and sat down on his feet. The mean looking puppy gave him a slobbery smile.

"Because he did it, that's why. He's been acting out since we got here. He even used my favorite boots as chew toys the other day."

"Maybe he thought it was a dead animal from the odor coming from them."

"Fuck you, man, I think he needs obedience school."

"He does not, he's perfectly behaved with me, maybe it's just you."

"You've spoiled him."

"No, I haven't. Look at his handsome face." He shook Herc's heavy jowls and smiled sweetly at Zerk. Zerk threw his hands in the air and stormed off. "You're so cute," he hollered after him. "Now, where did you hide Daddy's stuff?" Herc huffed and ambled away. He followed behind the massive dog. Instead of going to Zerk's room, Herc went for his and Landon walked in. The dog fell to his belly beside the bed and dragged the lost items from underneath.

"Zerk, Herc gave me your stuff back."

Heavy steps echoed in the narrow hallway and Landon glanced over his shoulder.

"How the hell..." Zerk asked.

"I asked him where Daddy's stuff was."

"You've stolen my dog." There was no denying the tone was vehemently accusatory. He had to admit though Zerk was an only child and not prone to share. It was pretty cute on the gruff, mountain of a man.

"How could I have stolen your dog? I didn't take him anywhere."

"He used to love me."

"Why are you pouting?"

"I'm not."

"Yes, you are. You're sulking. What happened?" He approached Zerk and twined his arms around the big man. Landon tipped his head back to look up at Zerk.

"Ron called today."

Zerk's biceps rested on his shoulders, and his hands absently stroked Landon's back.

I will not read anything into it, I will not...

Who the fuck was he kidding? Any way he could get Zerk to touch him was fine by him, even if it was just moments when Zerk needed comfort. Attraction or not, Zerk was still one of his best friends.

"Reconciliation call?" It took every ounce of control to keep his voice caring and not let his disappointment come through.

"He asked to meet, but I told him no. I don't want to hear what he has to say."

"Did he say why he wanted to meet?" He laid his head on Zerk's chest and inhaled the clean musky scent of the man's body wash. Landon held his breath as he waited for the answer. Someone spends over a year with someone there should be some residual feelings after the breakup. That was a lot of time invested.

"I didn't wait to hear."

"I hate to ask this," Landon hesitated.

"Ask whatever. You know none of Twirled Crazies have secrets."

"True. You were upset about the breakup, but not, I don't know, you weren't—"

"Devastated?"

"Yeah, that. I mean, you were with the asshole for over a year."

Zerk pushed a heavy sigh passed his compressed lips. "At first, I was flattered someone who looked like Ron—"

"What did Ron look like?"

"You know—pretty."

"You're gorgeous. He was lucky to have you."

"This is fucking bullshit. I knew it wasn't going to work."

"Then why stay with him so long," Landon asked. He squeezed Zerk one more time and stepped backward until he sat on the edge of his bed. Herc jumped up and curled behind him.

He watched Zerk shove his hands into his pockets and leaned against the wall beside the door. The muscles in Zerk's arms and chest flexed, Landon's gaze chased each shift beneath the tattooed skin and the thin cotton of his shirt. He leaned forward and placed his forearms on his knees. Zerk didn't realize what his bulky frame did to Landon. Having Zerk in his house was going to be harder than he first thought and he thought it was damn near torture already.

"I was fucking stubborn."

"You, stubborn? No," he said and grinned.

"Yeah, yeah, I'm done with him. Should I move back to Twirled House?"

"No, you're fine here. The guys are great, but you need some time to yourself. You know how they are."

"They already gave me shit at work. Why didn't anyone ever tell me how much they fucking didn't like Ron?"

"You're a grown ass man, Zerk. And just so you know, we weren't that subtle about showing we didn't like him. Come on, he didn't like the guys or the runs. The one Sunday night he hung with us you'd have thought he was being tortured. I think he actually put a handkerchief down on one of Scary's barstools before he sat on it."

Landon almost felt bad for laughing when Zerk huffed and banged the back of his head against the wall.

"Don't think about it just answer. Do you want to get back with him?"

"No!" Zerk practically hollered his answer.

"Good answer. You were settling when you started dating Ron."

"Settling? An investment banker who looked like a blond Adonis?"

"Definitely settling."

Zerk pushed away from the wall, removed his hands from his pockets and approached his bed. He held his breath as the big man sat down next to him. Zerk's weight caused him to lean toward him. The big man flopped backward, crossed his muscular arms under his head and Landon fell back to rest his head on Zerk's bicep.

"If you wanted in my bed, all you had to do was ask."

Zerk snorted and tweaked his hair. "Funny man."

"I try. You ready to have the house to yourself?"

"Going out of town?"

"My boss said I'd be gone maybe two weeks. I don't want to go, but it's the downside of my job. Some guy embezzled from his own company and they want to know where the money is before the guy skips out on his court date."

"It'll be weird being here by myself. Maybe I should just go back—"

"No, you're fine. But I'm sure Trouble would bring his baby to help you move."

Trouble was psycho over his 1957 *Chevy* Pickup. He'd probably cut one of their hands off for leaving a fingerprint.

"Yeah, I can see me scratching the bed, and my body turns up six months from now."

He patted Zerk's chest and tightened his abs to sit up. "Okay, I gotta pack. I have to catch a 7 a.m. flight. This is the only thing about my job I hate."

"If that's the only thing, then it ain't so bad. We're meeting up at Twirled House for dinner, want to join?"

"No, you go ahead. I have to pack and crash early." He leaned over and kissed Zerk's hairy cheek. "Have fun. Tell them hi for me."

"Will do." Zerk got up and headed for the door. "Landon?"

"Yeah," He asked as he pulled his suitcase from under his bed. He glanced over his shoulder and caught Zerk rubbing the back of his neck.

"Thanks for this. You don't know how much I appreciate it."

"What are friends for, big guy?" Landon asked with a smile. "Oh, and no Brawler visits while I'm gone. No one will be around to bail your asses out."

Brawlers was Scary's bar he ran with his best friend, Tank. It was rough, and fights were par for the course on the weekends—too much testosterone and alcohol. Scary and Tank ran the place with an iron fist, but to be honest, they sometimes were the ones right there in the middle. The Twirled and Brawler Crews were loyal to the end and always jumped into the fray.

"We'll behave. Our responsible members are going to be out of town, no Gib, Peaches or you to trudge down to the station at 3 a.m. to post the bail."

"Exactly. Now get out here. I'll see you in a few weeks."

Zerk exited his room chuckling, and Landon wanted to call him back. He'd waited too damn long for that moment, and now work was getting in the way. The sooner Landon got there and figured out what was going on, the sooner he could get back home to work on getting Zerk to see him as a man and not just a friend. He just hoped like fuck he wasn't setting himself up for disappointment.

5 CABIN FEVER HAS SET IN

Zerk stared at the wall Lucky painted to look like some tie-dyed, psychedelic acid trip and absently scratched Herc's head. The quiet at home quickly became unbearable without Landon there. Dammit, it wasn't home. It was Landon's house, and he was a temporary resident until he got his shit together. It was only three days, but it felt like longer. He'd sent texts asking stupid shit just to have some contact.

His phone chimed with a text notification. When he removed his hand from Herc's head, the dog huffed and ambled off to find another sycophant to worship him. Landon completely spoiled Zerk's damn dog. He leaned to the side and dug his phone out, and then checked the display.

Landon: *Miss me yet?;)*

He read the text and snorted, then replied.

Zerk: *Nope.*

Landon: *Liar. How's our son?*

Zerk: *Spoiled.*
Landon: *Not spoiled. Loved.*
Zerk: *Yeah. Yeah. Catch the bad guy yet?*
Landon: *Nope.*

Two damn weeks was going to feel like a lifetime. He'd told himself plenty of times to not get attached to Landon and what the fuck did he do; he got himself attached.

"Sexting with the boyfriend?" Lucky plopped down beside him.

"No, I'm not sexting, and Landon isn't my boyfriend." The kicker was it made him depressed, because whatever the hell his head said, his heart and dick wanted something else.

"Whatever you say, Zerk, but you've been sniffing around that ass for years. Your hairy, saggy balls just ain't big enough for you to take it."

"I'm not interested—"

"Bullshit. Landon might be oblivious, but we aren't."

"The man is just too damn gorgeous."

"He's a bit too skinny for my tastes. I like 'em fluffy. Something to hold onto."

"Like Priest," Zerk asked hoping to move the conversation away from him and shit he didn't want to talk about.

"Naw, man, not that I'd mind. But you know he ain't interested in any of us."

It was true, Priest was too skittish for the likes of Lucky. For the short year Priest belonged to the Twirled Crew, Zerk hadn't noticed the man paying attention to anybody.

"True."

"When you moving back in?"

"Someday, but I'm liking living with Landon."

"I'm sure you do."

Lucky's meaning was damn clear, and he swore him and Lucky would go a few rounds one day soon.

"Not that way. Living with Ron was like being in a showroom. Everything was so damn breakable. It wasn't comfortable, and it didn't feel like home."

"That's because he wasn't right. I'm sure he was a good fuck. He just had that look about him."

"Not really. Ron just wasn't into sex."

"Some guys just don't like anal. It happens."

"That's not really a problem. Although I love it, it's not the be-all of a gay man's existence. He didn't like anything. Hell, maybe he just didn't like me. Ron could've just liked the shock factor of introducing me to his friends."

"Like a fucking prized pet."

"Exactly."

He received another message, and when he opened it, it was a picture of Chinese Takeout containers with a tower of energy drinks and a caption: *Come cook for me.*

"You cook for him like a good little husband?"

"Shut up. He cooks too. We keep the same hours. He apparently doesn't sleep much at night. I don't know how he exists on so little sleep."

"Not everyone needs twelve hours of sleep just to function. It might be a hibernation thing."

He elbowed Lucky in the ribs as he replied to Landon.

Zerk: *You're on your own.*

Landon: *But… But… I feel my arteries hardening.*

"I'm sure more than his arteries are hardening. Tell that sexy man what you want to do to him. Put both of you out of your misery and fuck already."

"Quit reading my fucking messages."

"You're so touchy. That's what sexual frustration does to you."

He ignored the sexual frustration remark. It was true, but Lucky didn't have to call his ass on it. He hadn't had a decent fuck in forever and his gut told him sex with Landon would be anything but decent.

Zerk: *I'm sure you'll survive.*

He received another message and checked it.

Landon: *Be nice to me!*

"Oh yeah, man, be nice to him."

"Go the fuck away."

"Why you want to get nasty? Don't you need a locked door and lube for phone sex with the boyfriend?"

"He's not my boyfriend."

"But you don't deny the phone sex. Interesting…"

He snorted as Lucky stroked his imaginary beard and studied him like some science experiment. "You think about sex too much."

"You don't think about fucking enough."

"I'm not getting into a sex conversation with you because I still have nightmares from the last one."

"Prude, I'm going to bed. Can't sleep unless I—"

Zerk slapped his hand over Lucky's mouth before he could finish. "You can stop right there."

"I'll lick you," Lucky's words muffled.

He jerked his hand away. "And you'll lose your dreads."

"Empty threats. I'll tell Landon you jerk off to thoughts of him and I'll come up with all kinds of details how I heard you groaning his name. Don't fuck with me."

He didn't doubt Lucky. The man knew every weak point. It was like he had a sixth sense and Lucky didn't have any issues striking out when attacked. For a pacifist, the man was an evil fucker.

"Hey, what about your radical honesty bullshit?"

"I can make exceptions when someone threatens the hair."

"Go away, shit—" His phone started to ring and shooed Lucky away. Reluctantly the man disappeared. He stroked his thumb across the screen and pressed the phone to his ear. "I didn't forget about you. Lucky was being an ass, and I was getting ready to escape."

"Haven't forgotten about me, Brian?"

He shuddered at the smooth, polished voice of Ron.

"I thought we'd agreed not to do this." At one time, he'd thought that voice turning all low and husky was sexy, now, not so much.

"Agreed not to do what? We spent over a year together, can't we be…friends?"

"You know damn well we can't be friends in any capacity, especially not that one." The thought of it was distasteful. Soon after the honeymoon phase was over, Ron started acting like even the most casual affection was an imposition.

"Why can't we have some fun?"

"You never had fun with me and couldn't fucking stand it when I touched you."

"Have dinner with me. I realized I made—"

"Mistake or not, it's over. You made it clear when you left me behind in that empty house we shared."

"You can't tell me you like being back at that weird house with those freaks."

"Actually, I'm not living there. Herc and me are staying with Landon."

"Landon, I knew you were—"

He was learning one of Landon's bad habits of cutting people off mid-sentence. At the thought of the other man, he started to smile. Which if he admitted was kind of inappropriate now. "Don't even start that bullshit. I never fucked around, especially not with Landon."

"Oh right, because it's normal for me to walk into a room and see another man sitting on your lap or find a bunch of grown men curled up together on the floor."

"You knew damn well how the guys act around each other. Being affectionate isn't a fucking sin between friends." He didn't understand Ron's problem with the crew, and right then Ron was downright bitchy about it. "I'm done with this conversation, and we're not doing whatever you got in your head." Zerk ended the call without a goodbye. He didn't give a fuck if it was an asshole move.

There was no way in hell he was getting back with the man. The phone started ringing again, and he almost ignored the call until he checked the display to see Landon's name. He connected the call. "Hey."

"Berzerker."

Oh, man, that tone again. "Ron called me. How the fuck do you do that?"

"I know you."

"But one fucking syllable?"

"Yep, I have good news."

"Tell me, I need some good news. Ron fucked my night up." Ron didn't fuck anything up, he just wanted to hear Landon's voice longer. What the fuck was happening to him? That was proof he was losing his mind.

"I can't guarantee it, but I could be home earlier than expected. It seems Mr. Asshole CEO is pissing his pants that I'll find the company money."

"Maybe cut a deal?"

Landon sighed heavily. "He'll probably end up in a cushy resort for a few years. Off the subject of my boring as hell job, what have you and the crew been up to in my absence?"

"Lucky threatened to lick me."

"Are you and Lucky getting kinky when I'm not around to watch?"

His stomach twisted. "Oh, you're so not a funny man. I think I may've thrown up in my mouth a bit."

"You're so wrong, I'm hilarious. Don't be so damn dramatic."

He loved the sound of Landon's laugh but didn't want to talk about Lucky and licking anything a minute longer.

"Tank came in for new ink." Tank was Scary's best friend and business partner in the bar they ran together. Landon had a soft spot for the silent behemoth.

"Tank's running out of skin."

"The man is huge, so he has plenty."

"Oh, how huge is he? Are you holding out on me?"

"Okay, you've been spending too much time around Lucky. You're becoming sex-obsessed."

"I've got to be having sex to be obsessed."

"I think it works the opposite. You ain't getting any then you want it all the fucking time. Weren't you dating someone not long ago?" He asked the question, already knowing the answer.

Landon briefly dated a guy he'd met at work. It hadn't lasted long, but in Zerk's opinion, one date was too many. He needed to get over this thing he had for Landon. Every guy Landon dated was like him; handsome, intelligent and normal. Okay, Landon wasn't normal, he was just great at faking it.

"Don't remind me. He wasn't a bad guy, nice even, but just not for me."

"Maybe we need to take you to Brawlers when you get back."

"Oh no, thank you, but no. I adore Scary and Tank, but I don't want to hook up with one of their crew. They're weirder than the Twirled one."

"And that's saying a lot."

The Brawler was a revolving door of twisted dysfunction. If they weren't acting like a bad ass security team, they were kids fighting amongst each other. The Brawlers had a running pool on who would win the most fights, and the amount of the pot hit five digits' months ago.

"Exactly. I do know what I want to do when I get back."

"And what's that?"

"Make my first appointment."

"Why now? You've been waiting three years." There was something Landon wasn't telling him. The suddenness of his decision intrigued him, but he wasn't going to question it too much. He didn't want to change Landon's mind. Although, Trouble's suggestion kept playing through his mind. The tattoo meaning a claim on Zerk.

"It's the right time."

He'd waited way too long to get his hands on Landon's virgin skin. No one else would ever ink Landon. If it was the only mark of his that Landon wore, he had to deal with it.

"I have a favor to ask."

"Anything,"

"Don't be so quick to agree. Mom and Dad are taking their yearly vacation from the ranch, and they wanted to stay with me for a few days."

"Gladys and Roy are coming," Landon squealed. "They can have the second guest room. Tell me I'll be home before they come."

He practically saw Landon bouncing in his mind. His mother loved Landon, and the feeling was entirely mutual. Last visit Landon took a whole week's vacation just to show his parents around.

"Yes, they aren't showing up until the end of the month. They're going to fly into Atlanta, stay for a few days before flying out again to Paris. Mom's been excited for this trip since they started planning it last year."

"I'm sure. Last time we talked she was taking French lessons."

"When did you talk to Mom?"

"About a month ago, but she didn't mention coming to visit. The email I got from her a few days ago hadn't mentioned it either."

"They hadn't finalized dates yet. Should I be frightened that you and my mother call each other and email when I had no idea?"

"I love your mom. She's amazing. Okay, as much as I would love to talk to you all night, I should try to sleep. I have an early meeting."

He didn't want to admit how disappointed he was to have to end the call. "I have to get back home. This couch isn't comfortable enough to sleep on."

"Be careful going home. Give Herc scratches for me."

"I will. Good night, Landon."

"Night, Zerk. I'll let you know when I'm heading back."

They said goodbye and disconnected the call. He let his head fall back onto the couch and stared up at the ceiling that Lucky upholstered with some Saris his mother brought home from India last year. The dim light of the lamps made the tiny mirrors on the fabric flicker like stars.

He missed Landon being around. Travel was a big part of his job, but usually, he wasn't away for more than a week.

Landon popped into the shop almost every day. They'd sit around and bullshit mostly with Landon on his lap. Awkwardness never played a part in how he interacted with Landon. He'd had times where jealousy of other men took him by surprise.

Closing his eyes, he pulled up the image of Landon naked in the kitchen the day before he'd left. Landon had confidently stood leaned back against the counter. His pale, freckled skin stretched over lean muscle. His stomach was flat, not concaved or ripped, it looked soft to the touch, and he'd wanted to fall to his knees to press a kiss there. He longed to stroke every inch of Landon with his hands and tongue. What he wanted more was to see his marks all over the perfect body.

He'd studied Landon for the longest time until he realized Landon had his eyes closed and whatever he was thinking about was hardening his beautiful, slender cock. He'd taken several steps toward Landon before he caught himself and cursed his hard-on drawing Landon's attention.

Zerk pushed his hand to his dick and squeezed as he thought of bending that lithe body over the nearest surface.

"Dude, no beating it on our couch. Get a fucking room."

He groaned as Lucky's voice sounded in his ear close enough his breath fanned his ear. "Goddammit, man, quit sneaking up on people."

"Get your ass home so you can take care of little Zerk in private. I don't need to see that shit. Nasty bastard." Lucky's stomped away, and Zerk rolled to his feet.

"Herc, time to go home."

Nails clicked on wood floors as his dog appeared and headed straight for the door. He pocketed his phone and walked to the door, he opened it and stepped outside. For all the bad ass attitude and appearance, Zerk was scared shitless of Landon's rejection. He locked and closed the door behind him as he followed Herc to his truck. The huge dog jumped up into the bed and settled down for the ride.

He wanted Landon, but fuck if he knew how he was going to get him. Mr. Smooth he wasn't. Maybe Landon didn't want the smooth, sophisticated type, just maybe Landon had a thing for husky, tattooed and bearded bears. He could hope, but he sure as fuck needed to grow a set. Zerk just wondered if he could do it in the short time he had before Landon returned. He doubted it.

6 LOVING THE FUTURE IN-LAWS

Landon bounced with his arms wrapped around Zerk as he waited outside the gate for the man's parents to appear. He considered it fate that they arrived the same day he did. When he found out, he offered to bring them back to the house, but Zerk wanted to be there to meet them.

"You're more excited than I am."

Zerk's amusement was evident in his gruff voice.

"I haven't seen them in months, not since we went for Thanksgiving."

He hadn't thought it odd at all to go to Texas for a holiday, but he'd heard rumors that Ron was furious. Zerk's ex hadn't wanted to go. He wasn't going to feel guilty for it, and he didn't care if that made him seem like an asshole, he'd known the Andersons longer.

Besides he was and is extremely jealous. Jealousy wasn't an emotion he was used to, and the men he'd dated on some level knew nothing would come of their relationships. He was only twenty-eight, it wasn't like he was on a timetable to settle down, but if he was honest with himself, the only man he could see as permanent was Zerk.

"How much coffee did you have on the plane?"

"Their coffee sucked," Landon whined. "But I hit the cafe as soon as I got off the plane for espresso."

"I'm so glad I'm not riding with you."

"Hey now, I'm an absolutely safe driver."

"Brian," Gladys' smooth, Texas twang rose above the loudness of the busy terminal.

She waved, and Roy came up behind her, his ever-present cowboy hat firmly held in his left hand. Roy's gunmetal silver hair shimmered under the terminal lights. He was an older, more rugged version of Zerk.

"Oh, look at my gorgeous boy."

Landon almost lost it when Gladys threw her arms around him instead of Zerk. He hugged her tight ignoring the side-eyed glare he was getting from Zerk. Roy chuckled as he drew Zerk into a tight hug.

"Gladys, you're even more beautiful than last time I saw you."

"Kiss ass," Zerk grumbled.

"Don't be jealous. Green isn't a good color on you."

Gladys pulled back and cupped his cheeks, Landon let her look him over.

"I think you get even more handsome every time I look at you." She turned her gaze toward Zerk. "When are you making an honest man of him? You can't do any better, especially not looking as grungy as you do. When's the last time you trimmed that rat's nest of a beard?"

"My dog likes him more than me, now my mother has pushed me to the side and insulted my beard."

"Son, she'll fuss over you too, just give her a minute."

"You're so pouting. Landon said you have a habit of that."

Landon snorted as Gladys released him and stepped toward Zerk. Gladys was a little more than a foot shorter than Zerk, and the big man leaned down to give her a hug, then lifted her off her feet.

"You're looking tired, Brian."

"Got up earlier than I'm used to as you know I'm not on ranch hours anymore."

"You were always a night owl. Now, put me down," Gladys scolded Zerk.

"Have you shrunk?"

"I'll have you know I'm the same height as I've always been."

"I think you're fibbing."

She huffed and stepped back, smoothing her pretty sundress.

"Where's my hug," Roy spun Landon into a tight, manly hug.

Landon grunted as Roy attempted to break his ribs. "Hey, I'm not as muscle-bound as your son, don't damage the merchandise."

Roy laughed loudly and eased the hug before breaking it completely. "You going on a trip?" The older man nodded toward the luggage.

"I got off the plane an hour ago from a business trip, and I decided to wait around with Zerk."

"Are we staying at your place with Ron or do we need to get a hotel room?"

He did a double take at Zerk, he couldn't believe Zerk hadn't told his mother about the breakup. Their conversation wasn't going to be fun. Gladys' favorite subject was her son's inability to commit to one man. He knew Gladys wasn't a fan of Ron. She'd confessed in one of their calls she didn't like Ron. Being the friend he was, he'd tried to give Zerk support for the choice he'd made.

"Oh, Ma, Ron and I broke up."

"And why wasn't I told?"

"It never came up. It didn't end that great, and I've been getting used to being single again."

"You're being safe, right?"

Landon rolled his lips between his teeth before he let out a loud guffaw at the horrified look on Zerk's face. He'd heard the stories of Gladys giving her son the sex talk. She'd hit up every site on gay sex for her research. He'd nearly pissed himself when Roy told of what he'd overheard.

"I'm not dating anyone."

"I've been around roughnecks and ranch hands all my life, I know how men are, so quit acting so scandalized. Gay, straight, bi, whatever men are men. You always think with your—"

"And we're changing the subject." Zerk threw up his hands to stop whatever Gladys was going to say.

Landon loved the woman. "You're staying in my guest room while you're here."

"Oh, honey, we don't want to impose."

"Your big hairy bear of a son is taking up my second guest room."

Gladys' head swiveled so fast to aim a piercing glance at Zerk. "You're living with Landon?"

"I'm renting his guest room."

"Is there anything else that you'd like to tell us?"

"Why don't we get your luggage and get on the road. I promise to fill you in on the way."

"You better."

"Yeah, we better go, our furry son is probably depressed at being left alone." Landon grabbed the extended handle on his bag and turned on his toe. "I can't believe you left him at the house by himself."

"I took him to Twirled House."

"That's even worse, Lucky encourages bad habits."

He ignored Zerk as he huffed and headed toward baggage claim.

"Are you sure you two aren't dating, son," Roy asked.

Landon could imagine Zerk's expression at the question. If it were up to him, Zerk would be his shortly, yet he had to figure out how to get the guy to see him as more than good old Landon. They were going to have a nice visit with Zerk's parents and then he'd stake his claim. He just needed to be patient a bit longer.

✦ ✦ ✦

A big, heavy head laid on his chest and he scratched behind Herc's ears. He'd stopped by to pick up Herc while Zerk drove his parents straight home. Right then, Zerk was in the kitchen banging pans and cursing in the kitchen. Grumpy bastard—Landon grinned to himself.

Gladys and Roy were settling into their room. He lifted his head as he heard soft footsteps.

"How's our grandpup," Gladys asked as she stared at him from the other side of the couch.

"According to Zerk, I've spoiled him rotten since they moved in."

"Of course you have, but he'd already ruined him long ago."

She walked around the couch and took a seat. Landon smiled as she curled her legs beneath her, rested her arm on the armrest, and cradled her cheek in her hand.

"But he likes to blame me."

"Can we talk about something, Landon?"

"Of course." Landon nudged Herc aside and sat up.

"We wanted to thank you for what you did for Brian. Letting him move in here and all that."

"That's no hardship, I love having Zerk here. But to be honest, the only reason I let him move in was to get Herc."

He joked, but he could see in her blue eyes with the deep lines at the corners she didn't believe him. Was it possible he hadn't hidden his interest as well as he'd thought? Shit, did Zerk know? That would be embarrassing.

"Devious."

"I thought so. Where's Roy? He napping?"

"My husband doesn't know what a nap is. He went to help Zerk with dinner. I see you've domesticated him."

"He's amazing in the kitchen. The only thing I can succeed at is not getting food poisoning."

"I'm sure that's not true."

"It's very true, Peaches thought teaching me to cook was a good idea, but she quickly changed her mind and kicked me out of the kitchen."

"How are Peaches and Gib," Gladys asked.

"Good, they came back from a months' vacation. It's their anniversary trip. They travel a lot to conventions, but their anniversary has nothing to do with ink or work."

"They retiring?"

He chuckled at the thought of his parents retiring anytime soon. "No, I doubt either of them will ever retire.

Gib's hands are showing the signs of abuse. He lets the guys take care of all that now except for commission jobs, which usually means traveling."

"It's wonderful to do something you love."

"Yeah." He loved his job, but he didn't know if he could see himself doing it for the rest of his life as his parents were with Twirled.

"We had our doubts about what Brian planned to do with his life."

"I'm sure Roy wanted him to take over the ranch."

"No, my husband realized early that his life wasn't for our only child."

"What about passing the place down?" He knew ranches were typically passed down through families.

"When the time comes, we'll find someone to buy it, but we still have quite a few years before we have to make a decision."

"Not holding out for grandkids?"

"Brian has been clear that he doesn't see children in his future."

No, the crew sat around one night and talked about kids, Zerk was clear he didn't think being a parent was for him. Landon couldn't see kids in his future either.

"Yeah, he loves them, but he'd be great uncle material."

"What about you? Kids planned someday?"

"One day if I ever change my mind I'd give it serious thought. But at this point in my life, I have no urge. I might get a dog."

"You already seem to have one."

Herc had moved until his large head rested on his thigh. "Zerk's already pouting about me stealing his dog."

"Lasagna's in the oven. Here." Zerk approached and handed Gladys a tall glass of iced tea and him a beer. "And I'm not pouting."

"You so are." He winked at Zerk, and the man snarled at him. "Aw, that was so cute."

Roy took a seat next to his wife on the couch and Zerk plopped into his favorite recliner they'd moved in before taking the rest of his stuff to storage. It was the ugliest damn thing, bright orange with duct tape on the arms. He'd almost told Zerk to take it to the unit with the rest of his stuff.

"Quit showing off in front of my parents."

"He's always ruining my fun." He made a perfect impression of Zerk's pout.

"Lucky is your soul mate."

"Ew, don't be mean."

"How are the boys," Gladys asked.

He and Zerk filled her in on the antics of the Twirled Crew and some of the Brawler ones they'd met before. Zerk's parents told them about the latest gossip from home. It was all rather cozy almost like they were a real couple.

Landon shifted until he leaned back against Zerk's chair beside his legs and rested his head against the big man's denim covered thick thigh. Long, scarred fingers worked through his hair, and it was natural. He loved there wasn't an ounce of awkwardness between them.

Then he noticed the looks Gladys and Roy sent their way, but Landon didn't want to draw attention to it. He was enjoying the slow, gentle scalp massage. Too soon it ended when the stove timer went off signaling dinner was done. Zerk grabbed his hand, and as Zerk stood, he dragged Landon to his feet. He wrapped his arm around Zerk's waist.

"Let's have dinner, I'm sure everyone's ready to relax." Zerk dropped a kiss on the top of his head.

"I need to use the bathroom, I'll be right there." He stepped to the side and headed toward his room.

Landon needed a minute to himself. He was tired, impatient and probably had Zerk's parents speculating about a relationship that wasn't there. Just a few more days and he could make his intentions known. He just hoped he wasn't going to make a complete fool of himself and lose one of the best friends he'd ever had.

7 THAT ESCALATED QUICKLY

Zerk lifted his arms over his head and stretched until his back popped, then dropped them to his sides. It was only 9 a.m., it was too fucking early, but with the parents in town, he knew they'd give him shit for sleeping until his usual noon.

He walked shirtless into the kitchen scratching his stomach. Landon stood at the counter staring at the coffee pot. His pajama bottoms and t-shirt hung on his slender frame, and his hair stood up in all directions.

"I heard you coming." Landon's gruff and sleepy as he held up a large energy drink.

"Oh, man, come to Daddy."

Three steps brought him to Landon, and he growled as the man tried to keep the can away from him. He threw his arms around Landon and grabbed the drink.

"Your unnatural obsession with your energy drinks disturbs me."

Zerk popped the top and lifted it to his mouth, he chugged half of it with his free arm still around Landon.

"Just drink your weakling coffee and leave my choice of caffeine alone."

As he woke fully, he realized Landon was leaned back against his chest trapped between him and the counter. Landon's body felt just right against his, and it wasn't the first time he'd noticed. Last night when he'd combed his fingers through Landon's soft, thick waves, Landon had leaned his head against Zerk's thigh. Landon had seemed completely content to be there.

"Where's the parents?"

"I think they're still in bed."

"I got up for nothing," Zerk whined. "I'm going back to bed."

"Nope, you're already up. You want to cook or take them out to brunch when they get up?"

"Let's see what they feel like."

He backed up until he fell back into one of the kitchen chairs. Zerk closed his eyes as he mentally debated going back to bed or just napping at the table.

"Don't even think about it, big man."

He opened his eyes just as Landon set across his lap and laid his head on his chest. The man cuddled against him and nuzzled his throat. Landon completely relaxed against him with a long, contented sigh.

"If I can't fucking sleep, you sure as hell can't."

He brought his hand down on the curve of Landon's perfect ass. Landon yelped, and he smirked as the smaller man reached back to rub his cheek.

"It's not my parents," Landon pouted.

"Don't let Mama hear you say that. Do you need another one?"

"You going to snitch me out?" Landon stuck his tongue out at him and flipped him off.

"In a fucking heartbeat. Just a warning, don't stick it out if you don't plan to use it."

"Are you drunk? Let me smell your drink."

Landon made a move to grab the can, and Zerk played keep away.

"No, I'm not drunk. Woke you up though, didn't it?"

"Tease."

"If I were teasing you'd know it."

"Oh, is that right," Landon's voice lowered as he shifted and turned to straddle his thighs.

Zerk nearly lost it when soft, slim fingers combed through his chest hair. Landon moved in close enough for his breath to tease Zerk's lips.

Fuck, that was right where he'd always wanted the smaller man. Those slender hands fisted in the curls on his chest close to his nipples and pulled. His cock instantly began to tent his pajama bottoms.

"Now, boy, you don't want to play this game with me?"

Landon made a sound close to a purr. "Who says it's a game? Are you all growl and no bite?"

He moved quickly and bent Landon back over his arm rubbing his beard against the smooth skin of Landon's exposes collarbones.

"Is that what you want, boy, a little bite," Zerk rumbled as he teasingly nipped at Landon's throat.

He didn't understand what was happening. His brain was screaming it was a mistake, but he looked up into Landon's eyes. Landon's pupils dilated until the green was a thin ring and Zerk's brain short circuited.

"I don't think you got it in ya. You're just a big old teddy bear."

"I'll show you teddy bear, boy." He bit down harder, pinching Landon's skin sharply between his teeth and gripped Landon's ass so hard he hoped he left bruises. "If you wanna play, I can guarantee..." He stroked his tongue over the small red mark. "I won't leave an inch of your body without a mark. You wanna keep poking the bear?"

Landon squirmed on his lap and squeezed his thighs against Zerk's sides. He slid his hands up Landon's soft, perfect skin until he curved his huge hands over Landon's shoulders and forced Landon down as Zerk jerked his hips up. The sweet whimpering coming from the man on his lap set him off, and he stroked his lips along Landon's throat, and then nibbled at his chin. He was so fucking hard, he wanted to flip Landon over onto the table and ride that perfect ass until Landon didn't know whether to beg him to stop or to fuck him harder.

"So sexy when you whimper for me." He quickly pushed Landon's shirt up and over his head loathing the brief loss of contact. When his hairy chest pushed to Landon's naked smooth one, Landon trembled in his arms and held his breath.

Landon gasped. "Zerk," Landon moaned and rolled his hips forward.

Only two thin layers of cotton separated their dicks. Zerk lowered his gaze between their bodies and found the wet, dark tip of Landon's cock peeking out of the waistband of his pants. He brought one hand around, swiped his thumb across it to gather the beads that steadily leaked from the slit.

Landon bucked so hard he nearly fell from his lap.

"Don't touch me unless you fucking mean it."

Zerk's eyes jerked to Landon's face the moment he cursed. Landon furrowed his forehead, and his bottom lip was swollen and red with imprints where his teeth had bit into the lush curve.

Fuck, he'd never seen anyone look so beautiful. He sensed Landon's pleasure bordered on pain and was exactly what Landon wanted and needed.

He was damn sure he was the only fucking one to give it to him.

"Do you want me? Is that what all those touches were for—" He rubbed his beard over his man's chest, "those times you set on my lap? Did you want this?" He roughly shoved his hand into Landon's pants and wrapped it around the man's hard, leaking cock. He slammed his mouth onto Landon's to stifle his strangled yell.

How could he have been so fucking blind?

Landon's slender fingers knotted in his hair as the kiss devolved into a clashing of tongues and teeth. Their breathing rough in the quiet kitchen. He stroked Landon faster and sharper, loving the sharp moans and the way Landon worked his dick through Zerk's fist. He stroked his free hand down Landon's back and beneath the cotton covering the man's rounded ass, teased between his crease until he nudged Landon's tight, little hole with his middle finger.

"Tell me you fucking want me," he ordered as he broke the kiss, but kept their mouths together.

Fuck, Landon whined and jerkily nodded his head.

"No, I want to hear you fucking say it." He rhythmically tapped his middle finger but ceased the firm stroke on Landon's dick. Zerk needed the man to tell him what he needed. That Landon needed him. He tried to tamp down the primal, almost violent urge to possess

Landon in every way possible—his pleasure, pain, he wanted it all.

"I want you."

"You want me to fuck you?" He pushed until his finger breached Landon and he violently shuddered in Zerk's hold.

"Y—yes."

Part of him knew he needed to stop, it wasn't the time or place, but he'd waited too long. Keeping himself in check, denying his baser needs, but right then Landon was instigating the beast he always kept under control. He surged to his feet and slammed Landon against the nearest wall. Zerk growled as Landon grunted and tightened his legs around Zerk's waist.

Landon's short nails scored his back, at the pain, he ground his hips against his man's perfect ass. He leaned back as he brought his left hand up to curve around Landon's throat. Lightly he squeezed and used his right hand to jerk Landon's pants down until they caught at his upper thighs. He grabbed one of Landon's ass cheeks and dug his fingers in until he heard that beautiful whimpering sound again.

"Beautiful," he rumbled. "I could split that ass right now, and you'd let me—" His voice dipped to a rough growl, "Beg me for it." He lowered his head and bit down on Landon's chest, then brutally sucked up a mark as Landon pulled at his hair. Landon's slender cock rubbed against Zerk's hairy belly. "Wouldn't you?" He slid to the other side to leave a matching mark over Landon's heart.

"Y—"

"Brian, put that boy—"

Zerk turned his body to hide Landon and glanced back over his shoulder. Kill him fucking now, his mother hidden by the bulk of his dad.

"Fuck—"

"Watch your language," his mother admonished.

"Dad, give us a minute, please." He glanced down at Landon to find the blissed-out expression of minutes before driven away by embarrassment.

"Um—" Landon swallowed hard, and Zerk felt it with his hand still loosely wrapped around Landon's throat. "What the fuck—"

"If I put you down you're going to run, aren't you?" Landon opened his mouth. "Don't fucking lie either."

"Please, Zerk."

As gentle as possible he righted Landon's pants and set him down, held him for a moment until he knew Landon was steady.

"We're going to talk about this."

"Please, just let's forget—"

"No, go get cleaned up while I talk to the parents. Well, that's one fucking way to lose a hard-on. Motherfucker, I have to wait until my thirties to get caught fucking around." He adjusted his still half-hard cock and watched Landon follow the move. "I'll let you take care of it later."

"Bastard," Landon growled, but it came out more like a purr. He stormed across the room and jerked his shirt from the floor.

He didn't take his eyes off Landon until he disappeared out the door leading toward the living room. Landon might try to pretend that didn't fucking happen, but he lost his mind if he thought that was the end of it.

"Son, is it safe to come in?"

Zerk groaned as his dad asked from the doorway. He turned to find his parents watching him with a mixture of disappointment and disbelief.

Yeah, trying to fuck his man in their kitchen while the parents were in the house was an idiotic move. Goddammit but all he could think about was getting his dick in Landon's ass, and it was worse since his man bore his marks.

"Sorry, things got a little—"

"A little, my God, Brian, you were manhandling him, that was completely—"

"Mom, I wasn't hurting—" He stopped when his mother arched her brow. He wasn't explaining kink to his mother.

"If it's alright with you, if you and Landon could keep that to the bedroom while we're here that'll be great. I really don't need to see you—"

"It won't happen again. Like I said things got out of hand."

"What was that bull crap that you and Landon weren't together? You lied to me, Brian."

"Mom, I didn't lie. This is the first time this ever happened."

"Well, you make it right. I won't have my Landon hurt by your deviant behavior. I'm so ashamed, I should check on him. You left—"

"Mom, can we not talk about my sex life? It's uncomfortable."

"I should go check on my boy. Shame on you." His mom spun on her toes and left the room.

Great his mom thought he was some deviant. Well, they did walk in on him with his hand around Landon's throat. Fuck, that is embarrassing, if the guys ever find out he's fucked.

"I'll take care of your mother, son."

"I am sorry. This has never happened—never."

"It was a matter of time. You might be blind as hell but we weren't, and I'm sure no one else is either. If you want that boy, you ought to make sure he doesn't run."

"I know, but he's mine, and he fucking knows it."

"Let me go head your mom off before she tries to beat down Landon's door."

"Thanks, I don't want to explain this to her."

"You don't got to explain anything to me. But, son, let this be the last time I see your hairy ass trying to pound your boyfriend through the wall." His dad grimaced.

"Sure." His parents were cool as fuck when he'd come out in high school. His mother was a one-woman Pride march.

His dad disappeared, Zerk turned to lean back against the wall he'd had Landon pressed to and shoved his fingers through his hair. Okay, the truth was out, and he knew they wanted more than the friend's only bullshit. Although his dad was right, Landon was going to run. It was just a matter of how far Landon would get before he had his man.

8 LANDON'S ON THE RUN

Landon was in hiding, and he didn't deny it. He laid on his parents' bed and watched his mother put away laundry. Peaches wore a tank top and shorts that exposed her tattoos which covered most of her skin.

She'd met his father when she was eighteen and went to get her first ink when she went off to college. She said it had been love at first sight. His father had taken one look at her skin and said it was perfect for his ink, all peaches and cream. It's how she'd gotten the name.

They hadn't been apart since their first date. He'd always wanted what his parents had.

"Okay, cut the quiet act, you've been here for an hour and have barely said a damn word." She spun and slammed her fists down on her ample hips.

"What was it like when you met Dad?" He'd asked that question a hundred times, but he never got tired of hearing it. Peaches' voice went all soft and sweet with memories of her and Gib's life together. She never denied him and would tell it like it was the first time.

"Oh, darling, it was like a lightning strike. I walked into that shop, one look at that tattooed, bearded beast and I was lost. My friends thought I'd lost my damn mind. He'd picked me up at the dorm on his Harley." She chuckled and threw herself on the bed beside him laying her head on his stomach. "No one would've thought it looking at him, but he was so fucking sweet. After dinner at some dive bar in the middle of nowhere, we went back to his place."

"And the two of you curled up in bed and talked all night."

"Smart, sweet, and so sexy. He didn't push for anything and pretty much from that night we spent every one of them together."

"Did you ever doubt what you and Dad had?"

"Are you having issues with Zerk? We were surprised when you said you invited him to live with you. Way too much temptation for you."

"Definitely too much temptation. Things got a little out of hand this morning."

"How out of control? Gib going to have to bring out his shotgun to defend your honor?"

"Dear Fake Jesus, you're a smart ass."

Peaches snorted. "Come on, my sweet baby boy, you've never been good at hiding your feelings when you're around Zerk. Yeah, you take after your dad in the whole affectionate thing, but Zerk is your favorite chair. If you haven't noticed, he does lean back when you show up to give you room to sit down."

"It just seems natural, and I don't think about it."

"I'm not giving you shit for it. So, what happened?"

"Let's just say if his parents hadn't woken up we'd have christened my kitchen."

She snorted. "Remind me never to eat at your house."

He lost it and started laughing. Sex wasn't a taboo subject in his family. Communication was important to the Phelps. It was nice to know he didn't have to hide things from his parents.

"Don't give me that shit, I know from horrifying experience that every surface in this house needs to be bleached."

"Once you moved out, Landon, all bets were off."

He sighed as he stared up at the ceiling, "I don't know what to do, Mom. It just started off as our usual teasing, and then it spiraled."

"Did he regret it?"

He didn't have to think about it long before he answered, "Didn't appear so, but he's had time to think about it."

"You're doing it again."

"Doing what?"

"You're letting your doubts and fears dictate your actions. You've always been very open with us about sex, and it's not something to cause shame. You were terrified to come out to Gib even when he gave you no reason, but it was a second coming out since you swore you were going to marry Prince Charming when you were six I think."

"I know Dad had gay friends and y'all never balked when they brought their partners around, but—"

"There's no but, Landon, we know you thought Gib had the *it's okay for everyone else, but not my son* philosophy. That hurt him a bit when you were afraid to tell him. Hell, you had a bag packed."

"Not my best moment." It was one his more embarrassing decisions. The morning before he told them he'd packed his bag and gathered every penny he'd ever saved.

"No, it wasn't. Zerk's a great guy, terrible taste in men. We're surprised it lasted as long as it did with Ron and knew how much it hurt you to watch him with someone else."

"He's never shown—"

He remembered where he got his habit of cutting people off when they were about to say something stupid.

"He's shown plenty of interest, unconsciously and with great subtly. You're his boss' son and don't exactly look like the rest of us. Responsible and upstanding member of society, one of those boring nine-to-five jobs. For fuck's sake, you wear ties."

"Wow, can you sound anymore horrified?"

"Possibly, if you give me a minute."

Landon relaxed and wrapped one of the thread wraps in Peaches' hair around his fingers. The tiny bells attached to the wraps tinkled, and the sound comforted him.

"I'm hiding," he confessed with a grimace.

"Figured you were, but why? You're a grown ass man…take what you want. Kinda seems you and Zerk are on the same page."

"But what if he does regret it?"

"I doubt he does. Now put on your big boy manties and go talk to your man."

"I'm not just hiding from Zerk. Roy and Gladys got a nice little eyeful of their son and me this morning."

"Definitely embarrassing, at least tell me you two were dressed?"

"Mostly, my ass and well you know, were hanging out."

In usual Peaches fashion, she lost it. She had this great laugh, and when she laughed the loudest, she snorted. It was infectious, and you couldn't help but join her.

"I'm sure the future in-laws loved seeing that."

"Don't remind me. I swore Gladys was going to lose her mind. She came to my room trying to make sure I was alright, and Zerk hadn't—"

"I remember that college boyfriend you had, that boy left so many marks I thought you'd been attacked by an animal."

"Thanks for reminding me of that two-month mistake."

"Baby boy, according to you they were all mistakes."

"There hasn't been that many."

"Well, the ones you've brought home, they practically backed up and ran as soon as they got a look at the crew and us. You don't exactly prepare them for family night at Brawlers."

"What am I going to do?"

Peaches rolled to her feet and stood over the bed. "What you're going to do is get your ass up off my bed and go get your man. You've waited too long already. Zerk is one helluva catch, and some other man's going to snatch him up. And then you're fucked, and not—"

"And you're going to stop there." He stood and wrapped his arms around Peaches giving her a tight hug. "I love you."

"I love you, too. Call me later after you've sufficiently recovered to give me the good news."

"His parents are staying with us, can't be having too much of a good time."

"That's what gags are for."

"How the hell did I get a mom like you?"

"You got lucky. Now get out."

"Fine, fine, I'm out." He released her and strode for the door. She was right, his mom was always right. He wouldn't admit that to her. His mother was already too smug as it was.

✦ ✦ ✦

Twenty minutes later he pulled into his driveway beside Zerk's truck and cut the engine. He opened his door and barely got out before Gladys was beside him.

"Hi, Gladys." He slammed the door.

"Where have you been? Brian's been a nightmare all day."

He wrapped his arm around her waist as he steered her toward the house. "I went by to see Mom and Dad, but Dad was at the shop."

"How's Peaches?"

"She's great, getting settled back in, and Dad has a ton to catch up on."

"Brian just started the grill. We ran out to the store to get stuff for dinner. Are you okay?"

"Gladys, I'm fine. Embarrassed more than anything."

"Nothing to be embarrassed about. It was a shock. You and Brian never gave any indication you two were together. Not that we didn't think you were."

"Don't get your hopes up."

"Too late."

He shook his head and nudged the door closed behind them. Landon made his way through the house and out onto the back patio. Releasing Gladys as she pulled away heading for Roy, he turned his attention toward Zerk. Zerk was shirtless, sweat glistening on his skin and in the hair on his chest and stomach. There was no way he could resist; he'd never learned restraint when it came to Zerk.

"Finally came the fuck home," Zerk rumbled as he glanced at him.

"I went to see Mom."

"No, you ran, I had to take the parents to breakfast by myself. That wasn't fucking uncomfortable at all."

"The sarcasm is strong." He squeezed himself under Zerk's arm, and he shivered as fingertips stroked the bruise over his heart.

"Don't forget we still need to talk about that."

"Not now, especially not with your parents in the house."

"Why? Can't control yourself," Zerk asked.

"I've been controlling myself a long damn time." He admitted, and it earned him a rough kiss. Zerk's teeth worried his lower lip before pulling away. Landon wanted those teeth back.

"Fuck, I wanna see my marks, let's go inside."

"No, finish making dinner."

"No, we'll go inside."

"Behave." He wanted to agree because he'd behaved long enough.

"Why, you don't fucking want me to? Don't even try to lie."

"Zerk, let's wait until your parents leave. I'm not exactly sure why or how we let it get out of hand this morning. Just give me—"

"As soon as they're on the plane, we're taking care of this. Preferably you bent over the nearest fucking surface."

"I'm not going to jail for public indecency."

"Prude."

"What needs to be done?"

"Me, but since that isn't happening…"

Landon snorted and stepped away.

"Mom made a salad and potato salad, so those need to be brought out. Steaks and vegetables are on the grill. Grab some drinks, plates and silverware, then we'll be ready to eat."

He started to back away until Zerk reached out and fisted the front of his shirt. Zerk tugged Landon forward, and he held his breath at the heat in Zerk's gaze as the big man pulled the V-neck of his t-shirt to the side.

"You have no idea how fucking sexy that is to me." Zerk's knuckles stroked over the hickey.

His back arched at the pain and pleasure, he was so close to giving in.

"Go, or my parents will be having their dinner alone."

Landon didn't run, but he sure as hell walked fast toward the house. He'd always wanted Zerk, but after the morning, it was building to an intensity he didn't understand or think he was ready to explore. The tattoo was always about wearing Zerk's mark because that's as close to having a piece of Zerk he'd get. That wasn't the case anymore, and he didn't know if Zerk understood how important that step was or if Landon was just setting himself up for a heartbreak he wouldn't survive.

9 TO TEASE OR NOT TO TEASE?

Sitting across from Landon at the dinner table he observed the man talking with Roy and Gladys. Landon was perpetually happy and always looked at the positive in life, that drew him to Landon. Peaches and Gib were the same. Okay, he was satisfied with his life, and he was right where he wanted to be, but part of him was pessimistic as fuck. An enormous contributing factor was the year and a half he spent with Ron.

He'd reined in his dominant tendencies and hid vast segments of his personality to make a man happy. That wouldn't be the case with Landon. What happened between them that morning proved they were on the same page. The whimpers, the begging, and Landon's slimly muscled body against his drove out all rational thought.

Zerk never was one who could be led by his dick. Yeah, he wanted sex, he wanted lots of rough, sweaty and nasty sex, but he also wanted the one.

His parents were high school sweethearts. He'd rarely seen them fight, he knew they had when shit went down, and you could hear the two of them yelling miles away. They both had strong personalities and opinions, his mother was ranch and rodeo raised, his father was the same. Ranch life wasn't for the weak. Long days in the beginning with more times spent in the red than in the black.

Gladys was an only child, and her father treated her more like a boy. One thing he'd never seen was his parents going to bed mad. Things blew up, and they moved on. He wanted that kind of relationship where two people stuck together no matter how bad it got because they loved each other and could work through their shit.

He could clearly see that life with Landon. When the fuck did he turn into a sap—some hopeless romantic? It sure as fuck hadn't been in his time with Ron. In the end, they were acquaintances with benefits and mediocre ones at that.

A barefoot nudged his calf, and he glanced across the table to find Landon watching him with a raised brow.

"Your mother called your name three times."

"Sorry, Mom, kinda zoned out."

"I can see that. Peaches and Gib invited all of us over tomorrow night for a barbecue after everyone gets off work. The whole crew."

"Great, the guys were excited to know y'all were coming for a visit."

"I told Gladys I'd take her shopping tomorrow because she's insisting on making something."

"You don't got to do that."

"I know, but it seems rude if I don't."

"Fine, you can have Landon time tomorrow." He turned to look at Landon. "Don't you have to work?"

"Like I was going to work with them here. I took a few days and with being out of town, and the fact my boss worships the ground I walk on, he couldn't deny me."

He almost growled at the mention of the boss in question. Gregory Charles, for a nerdy numbers guy, he was sexy as fuck. Perfectly groomed with custom tailored suits, successful and irresistible if you were into that damn thing. In the past, a man like that was exactly Landon's type.

The grin that curved Landon's lips before the man sucked them between his teeth to hide it proved he hadn't hidden his jealousy. Fuck, just what he needed, he already came off as enough of an asshole on a regular day. Sexually frustrated Zerk was going to be an utter bastard.

"Knock it off."

"I didn't do anything."

He didn't buy Landon's attempt at looking innocent. "Yeah, keep saying that until someone is stupid enough to believe you."

"You're going to break my heart."

He rolled his eyes and took the last bite of steak, then pushed his plate away. Reaching for his beer, he slouched down in his chair and instantly felt Landon's feet come to rest on his knees. The man's compulsion to touch him still shocked him. Okay, Landon was just a touchy-feely type of guy, but once he'd analyzed it a bit, he knew Zerk earned most of the man's affection.

"I doubt that." Toes teased his dick, and he grabbed Landon's ankle to still the movements. The little shit was asking for it, but it would be best to deal with what was happening between them when his parents weren't in the house.

"Son, you two better behave. Your mother and I are going to curl up on the couch."

"Sure, go relax, we've got the dishes covered." Landon smiled and stood, then started to gather up the plates and glasses.

"I no longer live at home, and I'm still ordered to do the dishes."

His mother gave him one of her looks that screamed admonishment before she disappeared out of the kitchen with his dad following close behind.

"Your dad is always so gentlemanly. Apparently, you didn't get that trait," Landon said as he passed by him.

Zerk reached out and smacked Landon's ass, the man went to a full stop and moaned.

"You have to stop doing that."

"Why? Tell me you don't like it, that you wouldn't bend over for me in a second if I asked."

"That cocky ass attitude of yours is unattractive."

"If you weren't hard right now, I'd almost believe you."

"Asshole," Landon muttered and headed for the sink.

He pushed up from his chair and stacked the empty serving dishes. He carried them to the counter and set them down next to the sink. Landon started rinsing the dishes and organizing them in the dishwasher. He stepped up behind Landon and twined his arms around his waist.

"We've gotta stop meeting this way."

"Don't try to be all cute. It doesn't work with all that burly, ursine sexiness."

"Think I'm sexy?" He growled the question against the side of Landon's neck.

"Don't be stupid, you know you are."

He wasn't so sure about that. He'd always had a little padding around the middle, and it only expanded over the years, thankfully it hadn't reached full pot-bellied distinction yet. He was hairy and he sure as fuck wasn't waxing or manscaping. If some man didn't find some hair attractive, then he'd move on, but he'd wished he'd listened to his advice a long time ago.

The way Landon's fingers tangled in his chest hair still played through his mind. His little man didn't seem to mind at all.

"As long as you think so."

Landon spun in his arms and leaned his upper body back to stare him in the eyes.

"You don't know, wow," Landon whispered as his damp hands pushed under Zerk's t-shirt.

Those soft fingers working their way through the hair on his belly tugging as they went drove him crazy. Landon lifted against him, and he instantly lowered his head until their mouths met. He bracketed Landon's face in his large hands while fingertips played with his pierced nipples, and he thrust his tongue passed the man's parted lips.

He threw aside all restraint. Put all his desire into that one kiss that turned into a clash of tongue and teeth, hard nips. It was fucking perfect. He refused to go passed the point of no return and lift his man onto the counter and ground their cocks together. No matter how damn much he wanted it, the parents and his man needing time were the only reasons he held back. They were both shaking by the time he broke the kiss but kept their lips together. Their labored breaths mingled as he sensed Landon struggled with control as much as him.

"We have to stop doing this, it just makes it so much fucking harder." He jerked his hips forward as Landon slipped his fingers into the front of his jeans. "Yeah, that." The little shit had the nerve to laugh.

"We have to stop doing this because your parents will get another eyeful and one mortifying experience a day is my limit."

"I'm ready to fucking blow here, and you've got fucking jokes." He nearly came in his jeans when Landon's fingers tugged at his pubic hair.

Landon's right hand slipped into his jeans and cupped his cock, Zerk dropped his hands to the edge of the sink and took the counter in a death grip.

"Fuck." He hissed through gritted teeth and let his head fall back.

"Not yet." Landon nibbled at his throat.

"Unless you—" All thoughts of issuing threats ceased as the button on his jeans was released, and the zipper eased down allowing Landon to fist his cock.

"Perfect," Landon purred.

He was helpless to keep his hips still as he fucked in and out of Landon's grip. How many fucking times had he thought about that? Too many to count. Every muscle in his body was tense, his ass flexed as he worked his dick through the tight clench of his man's fist.

He snaked his arm around Landon to lift him off his feet and carried him to the laundry room off the kitchen, kicking the door shut behind them. "On your fucking knees."

With a small sexy smirk, Landon slowly knelt and removed his shirt, tossing it aside—Landon never took his eyes off him. If he weren't on the edge of his control, he'd bend Landon over for a spanking. The little shit knew exactly what he'd done. He shifted to widen his stance as

Landon tugged at the side of his jeans and pulled them down to the tops of his thighs.

Landon licked his lips. He groaned as he stroked his dick watching as Landon's eyes went heavy-lidded, glazing over. He cupped the back of Landon's head and painted pre-come over his lips, Landon tracked the movements licking up the trail he left behind.

"Open wide," he ordered.

Landon opened his mouth, and he slowly drew Landon forward, he groaned deep in his chest as he reached the back of Landon's throat. He felt the muscles convulse and relax as he pushed deeper. Tears formed at the corners of Landon's closed eyes and felt his man gag around him. He eased back then forward, repeating the movement.

"Good, so fucking good." He praised Landon as he steadily fucked Landon's mouth, he shuddered as the suction increased. Against his will, he thrust forward until Landon's nose was buried in his pubes and held him there. Landon swallowed around him three times before Zerk allowed him to retreat. His free hand cupped Landon's jaw and hooked his thumb in Landon's cheek right beside his dick. His man's tongue teased his digit and cock. "You want more, baby," he asked.

Landon hummed and nodded, Zerk's knees shook at the light scrape of teeth. Not enough to cause pain, but enough to tease his already overly sensitive shaft.

He looked down in time to see Landon fighting with his jeans until his pretty, slender cock was in his hand. Zerk couldn't think anymore, he wrapped both hands around Landon's head and fucked his mouth with sharp, shallow thrusts. Landon moaned with each pump of his hips, shaking. He sensed Landon was close.

Good fucking thing, he was about to lose his mind. He fucked Landon's face like he'd soon fuck his ass. He forced Landon to take his whole cock and held him there. "Fucking love when you gag for me." Tears slid slowly from the corners of Landon's eyes and down his cheeks again.

He pumped quicker, wanting to lose it until he shot his load down Landon's convulsing throat. His balls ached, his cock jerked, and every inch of him tensed as his orgasm hit him. He pulled back at the last minute, grabbed his cock in hand and stroked until he painted Landon's chest and chin. Zerk stared as Landon arched his back and creamy white seed covered Landon's hand.

Zerk fell to his knees, and he slammed his mouth onto Landon's thrusting his tongue deep, tasting himself as Landon trembled as his orgasm waned. He cupped Landon's cheeks and pulled back enough to take in the blissed-out look on his man's face. Landon's lips swollen and parted as he breathed raggedly. Landon was flushed and sweaty, so fucking sexy. He lowered his left hand until he pushed at one of his marks. Landon whimpered, and his cock dripped with more of his release.

Without taking his gaze away from Landon, he reached for a stack of towels and grabbed one, he gently cleaned Landon's face and chest.

"Weren't we going to talk," Landon asked in a husky voice.

"Soon," he answered as he nipped gently at Landon's lips.

"No regrets?" An odd vulnerability thickened Landon's tone.

"Not a one." And there wasn't, he wouldn't regret what he knew was inevitable. They were just fucking meant to be, but they needed time to think. This wasn't about losing a friendship for him, it was about gaining a partner. Whatever that meant to them, they both had to figure it out. Soon enough they could get into the heavy shit, For right now, he just wanted to memorize what Landon looked like at that moment. Because he was sure as hell he'd never seen anyone looking as fucking beautiful.

10 A STUDY IN PATIENCE

Landon stared as Zerk manned the grill with a perspiring brown bottle held loosely between the middle and index fingers of his right hand as he stood watch over dinner. He couldn't keep his eyes off the man, he was quickly becoming obsessed with Zerk. It wasn't a shock, he'd fallen for the brute a long time ago, but after yesterday, he craved the man's touch and taste. He could still feel the roughness of Zerk's grip in his hair, the hard thrust of Zerk's dick between his lips and the warmth of Zerk's come against his face, chest and throat.

He shifted uncomfortably in his chair and widened his legs to ease the pinch of his jeans on his hardening cock.

"You're looking a bit flushed, Landon," Priest whispered with amusement as the bigger man took the seat next to him.

"Don't start, I think the crew has corrupted you. Well, not the crew, but Lucky."

"That man is a menace."

There wasn't even a hint of anything other than fondness in his voice. He wondered if Priest realized how much he gave away even with Priest's usually stoic nature. No one had known Priest's story before he arrived at Twirled. They all assumed Priest hid some pretty dark secrets, but Lucky was quickly pulling the newbie of the crew out of his shell. Priest had only been with them about a year, but Lucky and he were inseparable. Lucky hadn't shown much interest in anyone until Priest came around. He was friendly and crazy, but Lucky was affectionate, almost loving with Priest. Lucky might be aware of it, although he didn't think Priest even had a clue.

"You know you're in love with that sexy hippie." He glanced at Priest to find the younger man blushing to the roots of his ginger hair.

"I don't understand how that man is still alive."

"By sheer stubborn will, I think everyone who meets him threatens his life at one time or another."

"I can see that. So, you and Zerk."

"There's no me and Zerk."

He knew what he hoped they had, but he didn't know if it would progress beyond some complicated friends/roommates with benefits. Maybe he knew and just didn't want to admit even to himself he'd been hopelessly in love with Brian "Berzerker" Anderson from the moment he met him. It would tear him apart just to be some rebound. That isn't the way Zerk seemed to be playing it, but Landon was terrified.

"Lie to someone else, I'm the newbie around here, but even I could see it from day one. You two instantly gravitate toward each other, if not physically, you two always search for the other in a crowd. Apparently, everyone's known forever they just haven't given you shit about it."

"Which is strange, because this crew loves to give each other shit. Especially Lucky, he has this weird way of divining someone's most hidden secrets and pouncing with some fucked up comment."

"I know he was raised with some kind of radical honesty upbringing. He's even taken me to dinner at his parents a few times. I can see how he turned out the way he did."

He almost laughed, Lily and Damon Trenton were about the most oddball couple ever imagined. They both had weird philosophies on life and how children should be raised. Lucky was incapable of telling a lie. Whatever filter ordinary people were born with his seemed to have been removed or didn't develop.

"Lily and Damon are great. You have to admire a couple that no matter what are completely and utterly honest about everything. I even heard they tried an open relationship for a while, but Damon not growing up in the lifestyle grew tired of it." He loved Lily and Damon as much as he did his parents.

"Do you think Lucky—"

There was something akin to fear in Priest's voice. A stricken look turning his normally pale skin ashen. "I doubt Lucky is a sharer. Are you okay?" Maybe a bad relationship, a cheating ex, he didn't even know if Priest was straight, gay, bi or another on the spectrum. Priest kept the hand he played extremely close to his chest.

"Yeah—yes, just got a little sick. It happens when I forget to eat."

Somehow, he sensed that was the closest thing to a half-truth as he was going to get. "There's plenty to eat, do you want me to get you something?"

"No, that's very sweet of you, but I'm fine. I can wait longer."

Lucky's long, lean body appeared blocking out the bright afternoon sun. "He hasn't eaten has he," Lucky demanded without waiting for an answer and pulled Priest right out of his chair.

The bulkier man was tugged behind Lucky protesting all the way. He couldn't help but laugh at the picture they made. Big, handsome ginger and the tall, skinny, dreaded hippie with thread wraps and beads mixed throughout his locks. If it was the sixties, he swore Lucky would be a poster child for the hippie masses.

"When are they going to realize they're in love?"

Speaking of the devil, Lily Trenton herself appeared from behind his chair and set down in the seat Priest vacated.

"You're setting your sights a little high there, Lily."

"My son can't do any better, he's a lost cause."

He inhaled the subtle scents of hemp lotion and incense, they were always the smells he associated with Lily.

"I had hopes for my least fucked up child."

"What about Lou and Linus?"

"Oh no, if Lou weren't the spitting female image of her twin I'd think she was adopted, and Linus is adopted, he's languishing in corporate America. Can you imagine the shame?"

"I'm sufficiently horrified, I bet you can't even take them to the family reunions."

"You do understand, I knew you would," Lily squealed and kissed him hard and fast on the mouth.

"You trying to take my man, Lily?" Zerk's gravelly voice saved him from searching for help.

He loved Lily, but she was way too affectionate for his comfort some days.

"Would I do that? If there were even an inkling this fucking sexy man was bi, I'd invite him to join Damon and me."

Zerk choked out a laugh.

It was a scary and well-known fact Lily and Damon shared in the occasional threesome, mostly men since Damon had come out as bi the night he and Lily met. The stories were avoided at all cost. His parents were exceptionally open about sexuality, but he didn't think he could handle them being as open as Lily.

"I've missed you, honey, you don't come around near enough." Zerk bent at the waist and kissed Lily's cheek.

She took his face into her hands and retreated to study him.

"You're even more handsome than the last time I saw you. You're getting laid, aren't you? There's a glow that only incredible, screamin' orgasms can produce."

"You just want details."

"Fuck yeah."

Zerk's eyes turned mischievous, and Landon made a fist, then drew his thumb across his throat.

"Oh, that's a new development."

Lily was way too astute and fond of announcements.

"You're devising scenarios just to fit your dirty mind."

"Whatever." Lily suddenly tugged Zerk down enough to look over his shoulder. "Look at that, I smell future son-in-law," Her voice went all wicked witch, and she darted around Zerk in pursuit of Lucky and Priest.

"No wonder Lucky's a menace."

Zerk chuckled and turned to lower himself into the chair beside him. "I sympathized with him more after I met Lily."

"True."

"You know I keep looking at that sexy mouth of yours."

Zerk gaze dropped to his mouth and leaned in slightly. He couldn't resist licking his lips, and Zerk growled.

"You're going to start that here?"

"Ya want to sneak out and head home? Because I have a huge problem you need to take care of."

He let out a moan/laugh hybrid at Zerk waggling his thick brows.

"You're an idiot."

"But you find me sexy and irresistible."

"I probably have significant mental issues from being raised by my parents and the crews that came before you all."

"So, you'd have to be crazy to want me," Zerk asked.

He sucked his lips between his teeth as Zerk's bottom lip pouted and started to quiver.

"If you produce a tear, I'll never trust you again."

"How do you think I got so spoiled? Mama fell for them big fat devastated tears."

"I'm snitching you out."

"She figured it out. She didn't think I was as cute when I hit sixteen."

"Um, I've seen your high school pictures, you were kinda—"

"Hey, I was awkward sexy, you would've so gone for me if we'd known each other back then."

"I was crushing on the quarterback who didn't know I existed until I drove my motorcycle to school, then I was the center of attention. Everyone thought it was so cool that I got a bike instead of a car when I got my license."

"I've seen your high school pictures, you were nerdy sexy, now a hot nerd on a motorcycle." He hummed obscenely.

"Perv," he said with a snort. "Are you burning dinner?"

"Fuck!" Zerk kissed him quick and then took off toward the grill he'd abandoned.

He went back to studying Zerk. The public kiss and him asking Lily was she taking his man, maybe it was more as he'd hoped. He was losing his mind. Zerk looked his way and winked while blowing him a flirty kiss. The man was fucking crazy, and he adored him.

"You two are fucking, aren't ya?"

Lucky's chin rested on one of his shoulders and Lily's on his other, like two demented devils who murdered the rational angel.

"They so fucking are," Lily answered Lucky.

He groaned as they cackled like two evil witches plotting deeds of twisted and epic proportions. He needed new friends.

11 ALL BETS ARE OFF

Zerk laid in bed staring at the ceiling. Twenty-nine hours, that's how long it was since the incident in the laundry room, and yes, he was fucking counting. He curled his upper body and threw his legs over the edge of the bed. All bets were off; he was tired of waiting. It was 2 a.m., and his parents were long asleep and needed to be up early to leave for the airport. Getting to his feet, he made his way to the door leaving Herc snoring on his bed. He opened the door and peeked from right to left to make sure the coast was clear. Fuck, he was acting like a teenager sneaking out of the house instead of a grown ass man able to do whatever the fuck he wanted to do.

Grown or not, he eased out into the hall and closed the door partially. Herc would cause a scene if he were locked in the bedroom. His two-hundred-pound dog throwing a middle of the night tantrum would completely fuck up his plan.

Stopping at Landon's closed door, he reached out and turned the knob, pushing it open. He walked inside, locked the door behind him and leaned back against it.

Landon was sprawled face down with the covers pushed to the foot of the bed. He'd waited so long to the point he'd almost lost Landon. He remembered the years of jealousy when Landon dated someone. All the fucking time he'd put into that train wreck that was Ron.

With three long strides, he reached the bed and leaned over to press his fists into the mattress. He lowered until he could nip at Landon's lower back. Zerk stroked his tongue up the valley of Landon's spine. His man groaned and lifted his hips. He growled as he laid down on Landon and took Landon's earlobe between his teeth biting down gently.

"Zerk," Landon whimpered in his sleep.

He inhaled the musk of Landon's skin mixed with the lingering scent of soap. His cotton covered dick rode the crease between Landon's cheeks. Landon's slender hand came back to wrap around his nape then upward to fist in his hair. Landon's rounded ass pushed up to rub against him.

"I think we need to talk."

"Really, it's the middle of the night, and you want to talk—" Landon turned his head, his lips brushing the corner of Zerk's mouth. "Now?"

He slipped his left arm under Landon and splayed his hand across Landon's smooth chest.

"Yeah, now, I gave you a whole twenty-nine hours to think. I figured I was generous giving you that long."

"I'm in awe of your—"

He pressed against the bruises he'd left, and Landon moaned. "You should be. On your hands and knees." He reached over and turned on the lamp, dimly illuminating the room and lifted to sit back on his heels.

Landon quickly obeyed. He palmed the perfect curves of Landon's ass, and fine hairs tickled his hands. Raising his left hand, he brought it sharply down and the sound of skin connecting filled the room. Landon arched and pushed his hips higher. He repeated on the other cheek, repeating the motions several times soothing between each one until Landon's skin was red with his hand prints.

"You look sexy as fuck with my marks on you."

Landon writhed and whined unable to keep still. He impatiently shoved his pants down to release his achingly hard dick. Zerk leaned forward to nuzzle the inflamed flesh and abraded it with his thick beard. Landon's moans and pleas muffled by the pillow. Any other time he'd demand to hear the hungry, desperate cries, but tonight a little restraint was in order. He pressed a biting kiss to the top of Landon's crease as he forced his ass open until he could peer at the tight, wrinkled hole. Fuck, he wanted inside—now.

He stroked his thumbs over Landon, felt him clench and then relax.

"Zerk, quit playing," Landon ordered and lifted his ass higher.

"Impatient," he teased as he pushed the tip of his thumb passed the tight rim.

"Fuck." Landon rolled his hips taking more.

Tight—just the thought of fucking that tight hole caused his cock to twitch and balls to ache. He felt his mouth pull into a smirk. There was something powerful about having a lover completely under your control. He eased from Landon quickly reaching the end of his control.

"If you don't have supplies—"

Landon reached out for the partially open nightstand drawer and pulled until it nearly toppled to the floor.

"Easy," he cooed blanketing Landon's body and loved the sounds his man made. The way he writhed and moved beneath him. He reached into the drawer to remove the lube and a new box of condoms. "Planning ahead?"

"Wishing like hell." Landon chuckled and wiggled until he rolled onto his back. "Fuck, I love all this."

Slender fingers combed through the hair on his belly and chest—tugged roughly, and he settled heavily between Landon's spread thighs. Their hard cocks notched together trapped between their bellies. Landon's firm flat stomach conformed to his larger, curved one.

Landon latched onto the side of his throat, bit and sucked as Landon twisted the bars through his nipples. He growled and ground his hips hard into Landon's. His cock ached and throbbed, he wanted the clench of Landon around him as he rode the smaller man hard until Landon yelled his name. Begged him for more, begged him to stop, and more than anything he wanted the man completely lost in what he did to him.

"I remember…" Landon hooked his legs around his thighs. "…the day I walked into the shop. All that sexy, hairy perfection, I thought I was gonna come just looking at you."

"You barely look—"

"Oh, I looked and lusted. Now, we gonna talk or are ya gonna give me that big dick until I can't walk tomorrow?"

"Your wish and all that shit." He lifted to sit back on his heels, he laid the condoms on Landon's smooth chest and opened the cap on the slick. He squeezed a bit onto his fingers and started to prepare, but Landon shook his head.

The sound of the ripping of the wrapper was loud in the suddenly quiet room.

Landon expertly smoothed the rubber onto him. A few sharp tugs had his hips jerking forward, he looked down to find Landon smoothing a good amount of lube around his hole.

"Now, please—"

His gaze lifted to Landon's to find his lids heavy and his eyes shimmering. Landon's chest rose and fell in a quick rhythm.

"Are you sure?"

"Oh, yeah."

"I'm gonna go slow so don't fucking complain."

"Would I do that, I finally fucking got you in my b—"

He pushed the fat head of his cock to Landon's ass and nudged several times before it popped through the ring of muscle. His hiss and Landon's whimper sounded in unison. Moving in shallow thrusts, he lifted Landon's legs to place Landon's heels on his shoulders.

"So fucking good," Landon moaned and lifted his hips.

He dragged his palms over Landon's pebbled nipples and leaned forward. Landon tipped his head back, and he wrapped his left hand lightly around Landon's throat. Memorized the quickening pulse as he squeezed gently and slammed his hips forward, splitting Landon wide.

Landon shook hard beneath him as he set a brutal and punishing pace. Landon's muscles slammed down around his dick. High-pitched grunts echoed with each hard piston snap of his hips, and he felt each one against his palm.

"Harder, fuck—"

He squeezed a bit tighter, Landon's skin was flushed pink and began to mist with sweat. Whatever control he possessed fled in the wake of his need for more.

"Wrap your legs around my waist, now." His body bowed with the force of his movements, and he lowered his mouth to Landon's, the kiss was sloppy as their tongues dueled. Nails clawed down his back and painfully sunk into his ass. Landon's breaths were labored as they came together in a mutual clash of bodies striving for release.

His size and strength were always kept under control before, but it was impossible with Landon. He'd waited too fucking long—too many years. He released Landon's throat and slammed his fists into the mattress above Landon's shoulders. There was no way he could hold back any longer.

He growled as he pushed Landon's ass into the bed and rocked him with the snaps of his hips. Drove deeper with each thrust, on one of them, Landon's breathing stalled and a cry froze in Landon's throat. He repeatedly aimed for that one spot as Landon continued to hold his breath and remained still with his hips canted upward.

That's when he knew he had his man right where he wanted him. Landon's mouth was held wide, and his eyes were squeezed shut. He couldn't take his gaze from him, and just as Landon started to throw his head back, he slammed his mouth down onto Landon's to muffle his scream.

He worked through the pleasure clenched muscles, forced through the vice like grip until he felt the tingle at the base of his spine. His sac drew up tight and his cock pulsed as he emptied into the condom. His body shook as he growled through each surge of ecstasy and seed that left him. Landon went limp beneath him, and still, he drew out his own pleasure, then collapsed onto Landon's trembling body feeling the quiver of Landon's thighs against his hips.

He reached down to hold the condom as he slipped from Landon. He started to roll to the side to relieve Landon of his weight.

"No, stay."

"I'm too fucking—"

"Heavy, fuck that." Landon's embraced him tightly as their sweat slicked skin reconnected. "Fucking perfect."

"Doing okay down there?" He pressed kisses to Landon's throat and shoulder, before tucking his face under Landon's jaw.

"No jokes, I'm fucking wrecked, I may never walk again."

"That good huh?"

"Fishing for compliments?"

"Don't think I have to."

"Damn right you don't have to. We could've been doing this for years."

"You seriously been thinking about this since we fucking met?" He planted his forearms on the bed, lifting enough to look down at Landon and stroked the damp hair back from his forehead.

"Before, I didn't even know your name, and I already mentally had you naked."

He brushed his mouth to Landon's small smile.

"I was giving off major signals. I practically offered myself up."

"You're the boss' son, and well, you're hot like a fucking model."

"No, don't blame my overwhelming gorgeousness on your lack of balls."

"I have balls, I just—" He snorted as Landon chuckled.

Landon's fingers combed through his hair. "We're gonna do this a lot."

"We are?"

"Oh definitely, there's a lot of surfaces in this house, and I get hour lunches."

He laughed as he lowered his forehead to Landon's chest and kissed the center. "I'm gonna get us cleaned up and then I gotta crash, you were too rough on this old man." He pushed up and stepped over the edge of the bed. Landon had a small en suite bathroom. He looked down to the sexy, come covered man sprawled across the bed.

"I'll be right here trying to regain the use of my legs."

He wanted too much, he'd had a lot to think about since the revelation a few days before. They were nowhere near ready for what his brain and heart were pleading to possess. He turned away from the bed. There was plenty of time to figure it all out later, so for the first time in his life, he was going to be content—enjoy what they had and not worry about what the next day would bring. He knew what he wanted, but he needed to wait until Landon was on the same page. He just hoped it didn't take for-fucking-ever.

12 BECAUSE GROWN-UPS UNDERSTAND BOUNDARIES

Landon shifted in his seat as he rested his sketchpad on his raised knees. Every station at Twirled was full except for Scary's who was at Brawlers, Gib and Peaches were in Atlanta for a custom job Gib was doing for an old friend. So, that left Landon to spend his Saturday night playing receptionist. They'd taken Zerk's parents to the airport that morning and came home for a few hours of extra sleep, then off to work.

"I hope that isn't true to life, because damn that would never fucking fit," Lucky screeched behind him.

Zerk growled in the distance, and he couldn't help but chuckle. He glanced toward Zerk's station to find him the recipient of a glare promising retribution.

"You're fully clothed, he's just talking shit."

"I better be," Zerk grunted out as he went back to work.

He so wasn't fully clothed. "Extremely true to life," he whispered.

"Wow, and you like that rammed—"

"Lucky, don't you have work to do," Zerk demanded.

He met Lucky's gaze, and they both laughed as Lucky walked back to his client who was taking a breather. The poor guy was in hour three of an outline for a full back piece.

He and Zerk hadn't talked much about what happened, well, they hadn't spoken at all. It had been natural to wake up in Zerk's arms that morning.

Gladys and Roy had already gotten up and started coffee. Zerk's door was open, so they knew he wasn't there. Gladys gave him an extra-long hug at the airport, and there was no possible way her smile could've gotten wider or brighter. She made him promise that he and Zerk would come for either Thanksgiving or Christmas.

He loved Zerk's parents had from the moment he'd met them on their first visit.

"Liar," Zerk rumbled in his ear then nipped the side of his neck.

"You're not supposed to see it yet." He turned his head to push a quick kiss to Zerk's mouth and turned his attention back to his sketch.

"I don't look like that."

Zerk didn't know how attractive he was to him. Didn't understand the power Zerk had over him—he owned everything that was him. He didn't know if either of them were ready for declarations, but it was taking everything in him to keep his mouth shut.

"I have an exceptional grasp of detail."

"You're taking a lot of creative license there, baby."

"Nope, a perfect likeness, every sexy, hairy inch of you."

"You and Lucky sneak out at some point to take a smoke break?"

"Haha, you're so not funny. Peaches was so disappointed I became an accountant instead of a famous artist." It was sort of a joke. His mother had oohed and awed over every painting or sketch he'd ever done. He knew a part of her hoped he'd follow in his father's footsteps and take over the shop one day, but he knew his father had left the shop to the guys in his will, they all—including him—had an equal share. Gib swore him to secrecy.

"Still not too late."

He chuckled and shook his head. "Only if every painting can be a nude of you."

"Wouldn't we have better things to do if we were naked?"

Zerk's arms wrapped around his neck and he leaned his head back on Zerk's shoulder.

"You do have a point."

"I have to get back to work. Quit showing my equipment to everyone." Zerk grabbed the sketchpad and flipped it shut.

"But it's so amazing." He made a grab for it, but Zerk stood and held it out of his reach. Surging from the chair, he jumped up on it to put himself eye-level with Zerk. He wrapped his hands around the back of Zerk's neck and drew him close. "Big and thick, all veiny, ass pounding goodness," he whispered.

"I can't plow my man's ass at work. I can't plow—"

"The employee bathroom has a lock."

"Away with you, evil one."

"Fine, back to work. Just a heads up, I scheduled appointments with you for the next three Fridays for my ink."

"Finally, you told me you were ready three weeks ago."

"I know, but then I had the business trip, and your parents visited."

"Should I take it down off the wall and stencil it out or would you like to do it?"

"Since I can't continue with my drawing of your magnificence I guess I should make myself busy, since I'm making the big bucks and all."

"That's right, at least pretend to do something."

"I was doing something."

Zerk rolled his eyes and headed back to his station.

"But you adore me."

"You're right, but I got work."

"So, now I'm a distraction, less than—" He checked his watch for the time. "Fifteen hours and we're like an old married couple. The spark is gone." He playfully stormed off to the reception desk and sat down in the chair.

"Y'all are so fucking cute, me and Priest wanna be like you when we grow up."

"Shut up, Lucky," Zerk growled as he passed him.

"Sex is supposed to make you friendly and relaxed, you're neither. Maybe you're not doing it right. You wanna talk about it," Lucky asked.

"He doesn't need no lessons, Lucky," Landon called out as he slid the ledgers out from under the desk and opened the accounting program he'd set up for the shop.

"I didn't sign up to be abused."

Zerk's grumbling made him laugh quietly.

If anyone had a problem with them being gay, they wouldn't have walked into the shop in the first place.

Landon's mother made sure there was a Pride flag right on the door. If a homophobe walked in, then they had to know they were on their turf. He slipped on his glasses and settled in to catch up on the books. He had three weeks' worth of receipts and deposits to go through.

✦ ✦ ✦

"You about done, baby?" Zerk's question came from beside him, and he turned his head to find the big man standing over him.

"Doing this would be a full-time job."

"Come on, we're headed to Brawlers for a few drinks."

"Thank fuck, I need one."

Landon saved his work and closed the shop laptop, slid the ledgers—which was his dad's old school holdover from the good old days. He loved his dad, but the man was a dinosaur.

"It's not that bad, I do try to keep up."

Zerk took his hands and pulled him to his feet.

"I know, since you started working here it's been better, but it still gives me a migraine." He leaned his forehead to Zerk's chest, inhaled the subtle scents of body wash, sweat, antiseptic and ink. He'd always loved the way Zerk smelled. After a run, it was sunshine, sweat and leather.

"Then we'll take a long ride after Brawlers before we go home."

He pulled away. "Deal." He shoved his sketchpad and pencils into his backpack, then slung the straps over his shoulders. He looked around to find the shop empty. Had he lost himself in his work so much he hadn't noticed anyone leaving? Apparently, he had.

"Hey, what's that about?" Zerk fingertips stroked the grooves between his brows.

"How long was I zoned out for?"

"For a while, we just sorta worked around you. Come on, the guys will be on their way to drunk by the time we get there."

"Scary will kick their asses if he has to drag them out of bed for the run."

"Definitely." Zerk looped his arm around his waist and steered him toward the door, "But we're done with work tonight, and now it's time for fun. No more thinking about numbers or anything else." He grabbed their helmets and held them by the straps.

He set the alarm and stepped outside as Zerk locked up behind them. Standing back, he watched Zerk swing his thick leg over the seat and settle in, he stepped up to the bigger man who was at his eye-level. He rubbed his nose against Zerk's then pushed his mouth to Zerk's, loving the tickle of the thick beard. Strong hands came up to cup his face, and the kiss deepened and heated up.

That had been a dream only days before. He'd never thought he'd have free rein to touch and kiss Zerk whenever he wanted. Landon smiled as he pulled back and handed Zerk his helmet, then slid on his own. He placed his right foot on the peg and mounted behind Zerk. He pressed fully to Zerk's back and wrapped his arms loosely around the bigger man's waist. The bike rumbled beneath them, and then they were pulling away from the curb toward the town limits.

The fresh night wind whipped around them, and he followed Zerk, moving when he moved. The smooth dance perfectly and naturally choreographed. He knew shit wouldn't always be easy, nothing ever was, but right then, he couldn't give a fuck about anything beyond that exact time and place. Everything else would work itself out later. For now, he was right where he'd wanted and needed to be.

13 AMBUSHED BY THE BITCHY EX

Landon's soft, wet hair was twisted around his fist as he bent his knees to change the angle of his thrusts. Scalding hot water pounded on his back. He glanced down to watch his thick cock stretching Landon's ass. Landon was wrapped around him so fucking tight. He'd already taken him twice in the night. It was never slow and easy, just long hard fucks that left them both wrung out.

He couldn't fucking get enough. The more he fucked Landon, the more he wanted. His sex drive had always been insatiable, but with Landon, it was all about possession and making sure Landon remembered what he did to him.

"You know how much I wanna do this fucking ass bare?" He sunk his teeth into Landon's shoulder and sucked hard leaving another mark to join the rest.

Landon's body violently arched and slammed down hard on his cock, grinding their bodies together.

"Watch as my cum leaks out as you lay exhausted in our bed covered in bites and bruises." He straightened as he doubled the pace of his thrusts, Landon's reddened rim flexing as Zerk took him in brutal jabs of his hips. Fingertip bruises marked Landon's shoulders and hips. The more marks he left, the more Landon clawed and groaned. He stroked his hand down the black ink that now graced Landon's ribs.

"Fuck, I'm gonna—"

It was all Landon got out before he felt the man's slim body arch and shudder, and Landon lifted onto his toes. He froze as Landon rode his cock, his rounded ass bouncing and then he was done for, he slammed Landon's body against the shower wall and emptied into the condom as he ground roughly into Landon's quivering hole.

Every muscle in Landon's body shook, and he knew the only reason his man was still on his feet was he was still buried deep relishing every fucking clench of Landon's ass. He groaned as he nuzzled the back of Landon's neck.

"Are you ever not horny," Landon asked with amusement.

"It's gotten worse since I moved in." He rolled his hips loving Landon's whimpers. "But how can I resist when I wake up, and this ass is waiting for my dick?"

"Only yours, fuck, sore or not I could live with you right here," Landon confessed as he squeezed around him again.

"If you wanna be able to sit and walk at work ya gotta stop."

He eased out, holding onto the base of the condom. He'd never been bare with anyone, never even fucking thought about it, but he hated using them with Landon.

The alarm went off in the bedroom, and Landon started cussing as he jumped under the spray and cleaned up. The alarm meant he was at the point of no return where he'd be late if he didn't leave in the next fifteen.

He leaned back against the wall and just watched Landon, he removed the condom, threw it into the basket next to the shower and stroked his half-hard dick. Fuck, he could go another round. It was getting out of hand.

"Take care of that yourself, I gotta get to work." Landon brushed a quick kiss to his mouth and jumped from the shower grabbing a towel as he headed for the bedroom.

Instead of taking care of himself as Landon suggested he stepped under the now tepid water and quickly showered. He walked into the room to find Landon already dressed and running a brush through his hair to tame the messy waves. He looked so fucking good in his suit and tie, he'd never saw it as a fetish until he'd seen Landon in a suit.

"Maybe I can come by the office for lunch."

"No, it was already embarrassing that my boss gave me an I-know-what-you-did look when you walked out of my office the other day. Let the heat die down."

"Bitch and moan, you gotta admit your afternoon was a lot fucking better." He pressed his naked body to Landon's back and lowered his head so he could rub his beard against Landon's sensitive throat. The man lost his shit when he fucked with his neck. It was a dirty trick on his part.

"I'm going to be so late."

"Then what are you still doing here," he asked as he cupped Landon's cock through his expensive, tailored slacks.

"Fuck, Zerk," Landon arched his hips forward. "I gotta—gotta go, you're evil," Landon hollered and took off like a wild animal was chasing him.

He chuckled and laughed harder when Landon flipped him off over his shoulder.

"Love you too." Zerk arched a brow as Landon turned on his toes and stared. Not exactly the way he'd been planning to say it. They'd only been together a few months, but it had been there a lot longer than that. "What?"

"You said—"

"I know what I said, now get to work."

"Did you mean it?"

"Of course I fucking meant it." He rolled his eyes, but then he had an armful of Landon wrapped around him.

"Love you too, you suck, this was a terrible time—"

"Work, you can bitch me out later that I didn't say it when we were in bed making love with candles and soft—"

"Oh fuck, I can't even imagine, okay, I'm late." Landon jumped out of his arms after a quick kiss and disappeared this time.

They weren't exactly the romance and flowers type. Their dates consisted of beers at Brawlers, long midnight rides when neither of them could sleep or takeout at home in front of the TV.

Herc peeked around the door frame and huffed at him. "I know, I know, Landon didn't make you breakfast before he left. I took up all your time, I get time with your other daddy too. Learn to share, you spoiled beast."

It earned him a glare and a growl before his dog disappeared. He couldn't go back to sleep. Landon screwed his schedule all up. He still went to bed midnight or later, but he was always up when Landon left for work. He knew sometimes he wouldn't be able to see Landon until he was done at the shop.

He couldn't believe a few months already passed since they'd made their relationship public the day his parents left. Quickly dressing for work and then going to fill Herc's bowl, the damn dog was a bottomless pit. He stepped into his boots, bent over to tie them, then straightened to grab his backpack. Hit the diner for breakfast and then onto work. Maybe work on some of the receipts to help Landon out. He groaned, the boring shit he did for his man.

♦ ♦ ♦

The waitress Heidi refilled his mug, and he smiled in thanks as he worked on a sketch. It was a present for Landon. It would be new ink for their one year anniversary, yes, he was thinking far ahead, but Landon loved the tradition Gib started with Peaches. He inked her every year on their anniversary with a custom sketch.

"Well, must be my lucky day." Ron's annoying voice sounded in his ear as slim hands rested on his shoulders and tried to stroke down his chest.

He pushed them away as he turned to avoid any more contact.

"What do you want?"

"Aw, don't use that tone." Ron folded his long, lean body onto the stool next to his.

"And don't act like we're happy to see each other."

"I'm happy to see you."

The pout he'd once thought cute turned his stomach because he knew there was nothing but a spoiled, overgrown kid behind it.

"Cut the shit."

"Never seen you up this early."

"I get up with Landon in the mornings." At the mention of Landon's name Ron sneered. Ron never made it any secret he didn't like Landon or any of the crew, but especially Landon.

"Still fucking that—"

"You'll want to watch your fucking self."

The man was quickly pushing him passed annoyed into downright pissed off. Ron could say what the hell he wanted to about him, but Landon wasn't up as an easy target.

"You've finished slumming, why don't you come back home?"

"I already have a home with Landon."

"How long do you think he's going to put up with you and your kinky shit?" Ron's expression turned into an ugly sneer.

Why the hell was Ron even bothering? Ron didn't like him, and he was sure Ron never loved him no matter how many times the man said it. Unlike Landon who he didn't doubt loved him even with their less than romantic confessions that morning.

He felt a smirk tug at his lips at how much Landon loved him and his kink. His man could come just by him sucking up a hickey on his body. He might ignore Landon and show up for lunch.

"Landon loves every second. Now, I got shit to do, and you need to walk away."

"You're turning me down to be with that cute little—"

"I'd turn you down even if I wasn't with him. You hated every fucking minute we were together. I don't even know why the fuck we stayed together. Just because you're a sore loser and now that I've moved on you're throwing a fucking tantrum. Landon's it for me, and you better get that through your head." He turned away ignoring the rage in Ron's gaze. "Heidi, I'm headed out, thanks."

"Anytime, Zerk, bring Landon in this weekend, Fran's making his favorite."

"Lemon Meringue, he'll be waiting outside when y'all open."

"Wouldn't be the first time." Heidi laughed as she took the money he left on the counter. "I'll be right back with your—"

"Keep it." He slipped his sketchpad into his bag and zipped it up, he slung one strap over his shoulder as he stood. Ron followed and stood too close.

"Thanks, such a sweet boy, you want coffee to go?"

"No, my energy drinks await." He turned away and headed for the door.

Ron was close on his heels, and he glared over his shoulder.

"Ron, I fucking swear, you better leave me alone. I was over this months ago, long before you left me and my stuff sitting in an empty house."

"I'm sorry, Brian." He hated when Ron called him by his name like he wanted to forget what and who he was.

When he stepped outside, he spun on his toes, "No, you're not, you could barely stand when I touched you. What the fuck do you think will happen if we get back together? Nothing, it would be the same. I'm done, and you need to move on."

"I can make it work, I can deal with—"

"Bye, and don't fucking follow me."

He turned to walk back toward the shop and was thankful when Ron didn't pursue him. He hoped like hell this wasn't going to be a problem. Tonight, he'd talk to

Landon about it, he didn't think it was a big deal, but he also didn't want to keep anything from Landon. He'd finally gotten who he wanted, and he wasn't going to fuck that up by keeping secrets no matter how innocent. Although if Ron was going to make a nuisance of himself, he wanted Landon prepared. If he knew one thing about his ex, the man had a mean streak a mile wide, and he knew exactly where to fucking kick someone when they were down. Zerk knew it a little too well.

14 OH SHIT, THIS WAS SERIOUS!

Zerk's I love you played through his mind all day. Holy shit, this was serious, Zerk said the L-word, and he'd said it first. He shook his head as he pulled into the driveway of his parents' house and quickly turned off the engine. Pushing open the door, he exited and jogged to the front door, opening it without knocking.

"You better be decent," he yelled as he closed the door behind him.

"Is this close enough," Peaches asked as she came out of the kitchen in her apron and nothing else.

"Why did I get nudist parents?"

"There's no shame in the human body, Landon."

He didn't want to get into the old argument of bodies being completely natural, and all were beautiful. Landon grew used to his parents' refusal to wear clothes around the house long before he learned nudity was something to be ashamed of. He'd sort of been shocked when he learned his friends' parents didn't believe in nudity being natural.

"Yeah, yeah, is Dad around?"

"Backyard and just as naked."

"I already figured that. I was only announcing myself so I didn't walk in on late afternoon coitus."

Peaches turned and disappeared back into the kitchen. He followed and then took a seat at the kitchen table.

"Thirty minutes earlier and you would've been traumatized. So, what do we owe for this surprise visit?" Peaches stood at the stove stirring a pot of what smelled like her awesome homemade sauce.

"Zerk told me he loved me."

"And?"

Peaches asked as if this wasn't a life-changing event. He'd known for a long time what he wanted in life, and that was Zerk. There were just some things in life you didn't want to hope for too much.

"Don't be so glib about it."

"Son, you two have been dancing around this since you two met. Is it freaking you out because he said it or that he said it first?"

"How do you know I didn't—"

"Because you were scared to say it and then not receive a response in kind. If that sexy bear had given you even a hint that he wanted more, you two would already be married."

"Who said—"

"Don't fuck with me. You want a ring on his thick finger."

"Doesn't mean you gotta call me on it." Peaches being right all the damn time was getting on his nerves. He did want his claim on Zerk to be visible to everyone, but they hadn't been dating more than three months. Wasn't there some rule about not throwing around proposals for at least a year of dating and cohabitation?

"Have I ever done anything else?"

"No, I think you started it when I first started talking."

"True."

"Landon, Zerk let you out of bed," Gib asked as he walked through the open back patio door scratching his bare, colorful chest.

"I need a break on occasion."

"When your mother and I got together, we didn't leave the bedroom for weeks."

"Yeah, that's why my birthday is five months after your wedding anniversary."

"Happy commitments don't have anything to do with a piece of paper. So, what the hell are you doing here and not at home?"

Peaches didn't give him a chance to answer himself. "Zerk told Landon he loved him first and our son is having a crisis."

"Son, don't break that boy's heart because you're not ready to—"

"I didn't say I wasn't willing to commit. It's just weird."

"What the fuck's strange about it? You two love each other even if you both were too fucking dumb to get your shit together years ago."

Leave it to his parents to be brutally honest. Don't dare spare the beloved only child's feelings. He dropped his head back and scrubbed his hands over his face.

"It happened so fast though. One minute we're our usual fun flirty friendship and the next the teasing gets out of control one morning." He lifted his head to huff quickly through his nose.

"Answer me this," Gib took the seat beside his and stared at him. "If you had the opportunity would you go back to the way it was before?"

"Hell no!" He didn't even have to think about the answer. "I'm being an idiot." He groaned and buried his face in his hands, then lifted his gaze to watch his parents stare at him with not an ounce of pity. He was so feeling the love.

"Yes, you are, but the question is why," Peaches asked and settled herself on Gib's lap.

"I don't want to screw this up." He placed his elbow on the table and rested his chin on his palm.

"You won't, you and Zerk were made for each other."

His dad was right, but he was scared. He'd never had a long-term relationship in his life.

"You staying for dinner?"

"No, Zerk had several appointments today, and Herc hates being at home alone for long stretches of time."

"You and that dog, won't we get grandchildren of the non-hairy version? Well, at least until Zerk Jr hits puberty." The query came from his dad.

"No, no breeding. Maybe one of the other crew will carry out your plans for Twirled World Domination."

"We can only hope."

It was an old argument that none of them took seriously. He wouldn't say no if his mind changed in the future, but he didn't see himself as the dad type.

"While you plot and plan how to get your adopted sons, minus Zerk, of course, to spread their seed, I'm going home."

"Fine, but Sunday dinner and bring Zerk."

"You know Sundays are for the guys, but I'll ask him."

He stood and leaned over to kiss his parents' cheeks, then straightened to head for the door. He was a moron. Yes, he freaked out, but it was completely natural. Not every day did the man of his dreams confess he loved him. It didn't matter he was feeling stupid because of his minor breakdown. He pulled out his phone as he got back in his car, and he tapped out a quick text.

Landon: *On my way home.*

He tossed his phone onto the passenger seat and headed for home.

✦✦✦

A plate was in the microwave for when Zerk got home, and everything was cleaned up. He curled up on Zerk's ratty recliner and flipped through the Guide looking for something to watch. Herc was taking up the whole couch. The click of the lock had him turning his head toward the door.

"How was work?"

Zerk placed one hand on the back of the chair and the other on the opposite arm. Zerk leaned down to kiss him, he tilted his chin up to press their lips together. He rested his forehead to Zerk's and lifted his hands to rub the man's broad chest.

"Lucky pissed off some good ole' boy who wanted an Iron Cross—"

"Even Nazis should know what a Pride flag looks like."

"You'd think they'd recognize the so-called enemy." Zerk crouched down until they were eye-level.

"How bad is Lucky hurt?"

"He got a black eye before I got to him. I left him in Priest's capable hands to be fussed at."

"Priest is excellent at that." Landon chuckled. They knew Lucky and Priest's antics well. The gorgeous ginger bear admonished the hyper hippie at every turn. "They're cute as fuck together."

"Don't even hold your breath on that one."

They'd discussed starting a pool for when Lucky and Priest would get their shit together. It wasn't as if no one assumed the two opposite men were already an item. Although, no one pushed because Priest's timidness made it feel like they were kicking a puppy. He adored Priest though, and if the two men were happy as best friends, no one was going to call them on their obliviousness.

"But they're so weirdly perfect for each other."

"We both know Priest has some serious issues, and he sure as fuck isn't going to let a crazy like Lucky near him."

"True. Radical honesty aside, the man practically screams mentally imbalanced."

"But don't we love that about him?"

"Yes, we do. I left you dinner in the microwave."

"Thanks, what you make?"

"That extra-cheesy chili hash brown casserole you like. Sour cream's in the fridge."

"You're the best. What we watching?"

"Countless channels and nothing to watch."

"True, but there's a gore-fest going on." Zerk took the remote from his hand and turned to a bad slasher flick they both liked.

The worse the movie, the better they liked it.

"I'm going to get my plate, I'll be right back. Do you need anything?"

"Nope, I'll vacate the chair when you come back so that I may take my usual post on your lap."

"You got it." Zerk gave him a quick kiss and headed for the kitchen.

It was always easy for them. It seemed almost too easy, and maybe it was, but he wasn't going to complain. They'd always just fit together as friends and finally lovers. Nothing was ever completely perfect, but he was looking forward to the fights, and he was damn sure the making up would be fun too.

"Move it, baby," Zerk called out.

"And the spark is gone." Landon got to his feet and let Zerk sit down, then he took his usual spot on Zerk's lap. It quickly became his favorite place after they met and three years hadn't changed it.

"Yeah, yeah, I'm the worst boyfriend in the history of boyfriends."

"Completely are, I should start looking for another one, a newer and cuter model."

"Fuck you, you love me, you said it, and now you're stuck with me."

"I am, now eat your damn dinner so I can snuggle and play with your beard while I try to tempt you into taking advantage of me."

"Your wish and all that shit."

"You're so sweet," he grumbled.

He lifted his arm to cradle his head on his bicep as they watched a movie and Zerk ate. It didn't get much better than that.

15 DAMMIT, DID HE HAVE A STALKER?

What the fuck, he stared across the street watching Ron sitting on a bench across the street staring at the shop. He'd already ignored five phone calls and a so-called accidental run in at the grocery story. If he didn't think it was beneath Ron, he'd think Ron was stalking him.

"Still got a fan I see. Must have laid the D pretty good. Didn't know big men had that—"

"Finish that statement, Lucky, and I'll stuff you in the dumpster out back."

"So, cranky. I still say plentiful sex should make you more relaxed. Has Landon wised up and decided to break up with you?"

"Landon and I are just fine. Ron's making himself a fucking nuisance though. He made it clear I wouldn't fit in his new life."

Trouble plopped down beside him. "Man, you're a great catch maybe he realized his mistake or whatever, or he's just gotten desperate."

"Now, I'm going to get it from the both of you?"

"No, definitely cuddly enough and you got a sexy ass, but you're like a brother and that's just wrong." Lucky shuddered and took a seat on Zerk's other side.

"Why the fuck would you ever…never say that again."

"Definitely not, I may need Priest cuddles so I can find my happy place."

"You ever going to tell Priest—"

"Not up for discussion."

"This isn't getting us anywhere." Trouble snapped his fingers between them. "Have you told him you're not interested and you're dating Landon?"

"Of course I did. Said to me I'd grow tired of slumming and come back to him." He shoved his fingers through his hair and tugged at the thick strands.

"He had to know you and Landon were a sure thing. I mean, fuck, man, you and Landon can't stay away from each other when you're in the same damn room." Trouble leaned back and propped his booted feet on the coffee table.

"Yeah, that came up in a conversation. Nothing happened though until after Ron broke up with me. Landon and I were safely in the friend zone."

"No, you weren't," Lucky barked out. "Dude, the first time I saw you two, I totally thought you two were fucking until I saw Landon bring that guy he was dating in."

"You three done with gossiping, or you coming to the bar?" Scary stopped in front of them putting his jacket on.

Scary was six-feet-eight-inches of perpetually pissed off man. If Scary wasn't one of his best friends, he'd be terrified of him. Scary's life was about three things, ink, fighting and fucking, he didn't give a shit about much of anything else. To be honest, Scary gave some prime advice, so he might have to get a minute with him to ask what to do about the Ron situation.

"We're in," Trouble and Lucky said in unison and surged to their feet.

"Priest?" Scary looked at Lucky.

"Naw, man, he said he was gonna just relax at home tonight." Lucky slipped on his backpack and went to stand beside the door, quickly joined by Trouble.

"Let me call Landon and see what he's up to, but he's been putting in a lot of hours on a new account."

"Okay, we'll wait outside."

They left him alone as he pulled his phone from his back pocket and quickly hit the speed dial for Landon.

"Hey, what are you up to?"

He could hear the smile in Landon's voice. He loved how Landon seemed to brighten when he didn't do anything more than walk into a room. Not with any of his past boyfriends or friends with benefits did he have someone who was just happy to be around him. They didn't have to be doing anything special. Sitting around watching a movie or simply having dinner, it was enough they were together.

"Heading out to Brawlers, want to join?"

"No, I've got at least another hour before I can get out of here. Go have fun with the guys."

"You sure? I can go home and make you dinner."

"No reason to wait around the house for me. Just because we're a couple now doesn't mean—"

"Yeah, yeah, you just want the house to yourself."

"You know it." Landon laughter filled his ear.

"I'm so not feeling the love. Weren't you just saying not long ago that the spark was gone."

"The spark's fine, but I'm not the clingy type, and I know you won't fuck around. Jealousy is also not in my nature."

"I know that. So, no way I can talk you into meeting us there?"

"You probably could, but I'm not. Just be careful coming home and make sure I don't get called to bail y'all out."

"We're not that bad."

"You're like big kids when the crew gets together."

"Okay, I've got Scary glaring at me through the window. Love you."

"Love you too and have fun."

He disconnected the call and grabbed his jacket from the coat rack. He set the alarm, locked the door, and closed it behind him. Within minutes they were speeding out of town toward Brawlers.

♦ ♦ ♦

Landon was asleep with the sheet bunched around his waist. He leaned his shoulder against the door to watch his man sleep. It was weird to come home and have Landon already in bed, but it was after midnight. Several times he'd thought he'd seen Ron in the crowd, but it had to be a moment of paranoia.

Not even to fuck with him would Ron show up a place like Brawlers. He swore the fucker was stalking him though. He laughed at himself as he reached over his head and fisted the back of his shirt to pull it over his head. Zerk tossed it in the laundry basket as he passed. He stopped beside the bed and stripped off his jeans, then crawled in naked beside Landon.

He gathered Landon's warm body to him.

"You're home," Landon mumbled and nuzzled his chest.

"Didn't think I would be?"

"Shut up, I just thought you and the boys would close it down."

Soft, yet strong hands rubbed his chest and stomach, his dick went instantly hard and rubbed against Landon's stomach. Landon kissed him; Landon's tongue traced his lips to tease him.

"Not too tired," he asked as he rolled to his back and brought Landon with him.

"For you, never," Landon moaned and straddled his waist.

He watched Landon straighten to look down at him.

"I can't believe you're finally mine." Landon's hands massaged his stomach.

He didn't even bother trying to suck it in like he would've in the past. Landon loved every inch of him. He stroked his palms along Landon's hairy thighs to his hips and massaged the creases where thighs met groin. The neatly trimmed curls tickled his thumbs. Landon's hips slowly rolled forward, the crease of Landon's ass rode his hard shaft. Landon shuddered atop him as he repeated the slow glide. He squeezed Landon's slim hips and held him still as he lifted his own to grind to Landon's hole.

"Why the fuck can't I get enough? Where the fuck is the—"

Before he could finish the question, a foil packet appeared in front of his face.

"Prepared," he asked as he tried to take the condom, but Landon moved it out of his reach.

Landon lifted and moved backward to sit astride his calves.

"When it comes to you, always." A sexy smirk curved Landon's lips.

He curled up slightly, then reached out to wrap his hands around the back of Landon's neck, "Suck me," he growled as Landon quickly obeyed.

He'd watched Landon's lips part seconds before Landon swallowed him to the root. He released Landon, pulling the pillow under his head and groaned as Landon bobbed up and down his dick, suctioning hard on the upstroke. His fucking toes curled as he flexed his ass and tried to follow the ecstasy of Landon's mouth.

"That's right, baby, swallow all of it." Sweat broke out on his skin as Landon worked his dick in alternating fast and slow, shallow and taking him down his throat.

He wasn't fucking ready to come, not until he was buried deep in Landon's ass. His man riding him. He searched the bed for the bottle of lube. His hand wrapped around it and flipped open the cap with his thumb.

"Turn around here, let me—"

"Already taken care of," Landon spoke as he quickly rolled the rubber on and slid up his body.

Landon's breath teased his mouth as Landon took the bottle, reaching behind him. He felt the dulled caress of Landon's fingertips.

"I hate these fucking things," he growled.

"A doctor visit in our near future."

"Definitely—" He sunk his fingers into Landon's ass as Landon's hole closed around him. The squeeze was unbelievable. It got better every fucking time. He bent his knees and planted his feet flat on the mattress.

With Landon's ass cheeks in a bruising grip, he held Landon still as he pounded into him. His man's beautiful little grunts against his mouth urged him on, and he took him harder and faster. He forced Landon to take more and more until his movements were rocking the bed, banging the headboard against the wall.

Landon pushed his hand between them and started jacking his dick in rough strokes, Landon's knuckles rubbing against his stomach.

"You better—" Landon threw his head back as wet heat spread across his skin and Landon's body bowed.

Landon's forehead pressed to his chin as a long moan combined with his labored breaths until he lost it. He slammed Landon down on him as he filled the condom. Landon collapsed on his chest.

"Next time you better be bare."

At Landon's statement, he jerked inside Landon a few more times. He closed his eyes as he tried to catch his breath. Landon's fingers gripped the base of the condom and lifted, he groaned at the loss of tightness and heat. Their cocks notched together as Landon laid flat on him.

They didn't say anything, just held each other as they let their bodies cool. He felt himself drifting off and tapped Landon's hip. "Let me get us cleaned—"

He chuckled at the soft snore. He eased Landon off him and rolled from the bed. Zerk stood there and watched Landon for a few minutes. Forcing himself away from the sight of Landon in what he was coming to consider their bed and headed for the bathroom. He quickly removed the rubber and jumped into the shower. He didn't want to be away from Landon longer than necessary. He was finally where he fucking wanted to be, and there was no way he was screwing that up.

16 HE'S ABOUT TO LOSE HIS JOB

The numbers started to swirl in front of his eyes. He loved his job, but he needed a vacation. A knock on his office door brought his attention away from his laptop and found his friend and boss Gregory framed in the open doorway. The guy never looked mussed. His dark hair always perfectly styled, his suits impeccable and expensive. Although he'd noticed dark circles under Gregory's eyes recently and a new tightness to his full lips

"Please, don't tell me I've got to go out of town again," he whined and caused the man to laugh.

"No, no out of town jobs, but I do have a favor to ask."

"Sure, what do you need?"

"Arnold is taking me out of town at the end of the month for our anniversary. Would you be willing to take over for me while I'm gone?"

"Of course, and I promise not to let the power go to my head."

"Thanks, Landon, I wish I was able to give you more notice."

"A few weeks' notice is plenty. Where's the husband taking you?"

He'd met Arnold a handful of times in all the time he'd worked for Gregory. Even though the two men were similar in appearance, he couldn't quite picture them together. He understood some couples weren't into public displays, but he'd never even seen Arnold touch Gregory casually. What he found troublesome about the couple was the way Gregory held himself when Arnold was around. A stiffness to his slim body and wariness in his eyes. He didn't think the marriage was a happy one.

"Paris, well, it's an anniversary and business trip, but I can do some sightseeing while he goes to a few meetings."

"Zerk's parents went to France for their anniversary a few months ago."

"How are things going with Zerk? I haven't seen him in a while."

"I've banned him from the office."

Gregory didn't have to say anything because it was there in the smirk on his gorgeous face. The tension of minutes before disappeared at the impish expression which seemed out of place on a man so polished and professional. It was like the Gregory he'd first met at his interview.

"You did look awful flushed last time he left."

"Don't remind me. Zerk's doing well though. The shop's busy as always, and they're getting ready to draw straws to see who's going to a few conventions this summer."

"Do you want time off if Zerk goes?"

"Maybe, we'll see how it goes. Hey, we're getting together at Brawlers Saturday for a few drinks, why don't you and Arnold join us?"

"Thank you, Landon, but Brawlers isn't exactly our style," Gregory cringed. "I didn't mean it like that, don't be offended."

"Relax, even though Tank and Scary run a pretty tight ship, things tend to get out of hand sometimes. But where else can you get ringside seats for free?"

"Maybe I'll talk to Arnold, but we can't make it this weekend. Dinner with his parents."

"Just let me know when you're free—"

"Mr. Phelps, there's a gentleman here to see you. I don't have him scheduled for an appointment." The receptionist peeked around Gregory's shoulder.

Landon knew it wasn't Zerk, Ellen knew him.

"I'll let you go so you can take care of that. Thanks, we'll have lunch and discuss what needs to be done, the appointments I can reschedule or the ones which can't."

"Of course, just let me know when." Landon stood and walked around his desk.

Gregory disappeared, and Ellen followed him. He strode out of his office. He groaned at the familiar man standing in the waiting area. The one man who could ruin a perfectly pleasant day. Ron turned toward him, and the smile on his face made his skin crawl.

"Ron, what can I help you with today?"

This was his place of employment, so he had to pretend at least to be professional. He'd prefer to flip the guy off and turn on his toes to head back to work.

"Landon, I was just in the area and remembered you worked here. I was wondering if you'd like to have lunch. Brian—"

"He prefers Zerk."

Ron snarled his lip but tried to hide it behind one of his perfect smiles.

"As I was saying, *Brian*..." He emphasized the name. "And I didn't part on the greatest of terms, but I felt—"

"Let me interrupt you there, if you even attempt to say that isn't a reason we shouldn't be friends, I won't mind losing my job today."

All pretense disappeared as Ron realized his charm wasn't going to work on him. He didn't know why Ron tried it in the first damn place.

"You know you're just a rebound, we were together for over a year. This separation is a mistake, and he'll realize it. We had breakfast the other morning—"

"Again, let me stop you, he was having breakfast, and you interrupted. Now, if you're trying to piss me off, it's not going to work. So that you know, Zerk tells me everything and I mean everything."

Ron's face turned red with anger, and Landon just smiled. He wasn't going to have Ron's bullshit ruin what he had with Zerk. The jealous shit hadn't realized the prize he had, and now Ron was regretting it. That wasn't his problem, Zerk was his.

"How long do you think you can pretend to like that freak?"

"For someone who thinks Zerk's a freak you're sure making yourself visible wherever Zerk is. Don't embarrass yourself further. You're not going to piss me off or cause me to be jealous. I trust Zerk inexplicably."

"You'll learn no man can be trusted."

"I don't know the type of people you've dated, but I assure you they weren't the right ones. Zerk is one of the good ones and you screwed up, your fuck up is my gain.

Now, if you'll excuse me, I do have to get back to work so I can get home to my man."

He didn't bother giving the man another second of his attention and turned on his toes to head back to his office. He already had his phone out and calling Zerk.

"Miss me already? Want a lunch date?" Zerk's question had him chuckling.

"I think you have a stalker or we have a stalker."

"What the fuck are you talking about?"

He closed his door behind him and strode around his desk to take a seat. "Ron just showed up at my office, he tried to make me jealous."

"He doesn't know you very well, does he?"

"Apparently not."

"This fucker is gonna make himself a nuisance."

Zerk tried to keep his tone light, but Landon knew his man too well, and his easy-tempered man was pissed.

"Don't get yourself into trouble over this. The man just realized his mistake. He figured out he gave up the perfect man."

Zerk snorted. "Nowhere near perfect."

"For me, you are, every freaky, husky inch of you. Speaking of inches, did you make—"

"Yes, I made an appointment for tomorrow morning. I'm heading over there before work. What about you?"

"I hit the clinic today. I took an early lunch."

"Impatient."

"You have no idea. Want to go out for dinner tonight?"

"Sure, meet up or head out after you get home and cleaned up?"

"I'll come home, shower and then we can go out."

"Okay, I better get back to work. See you tonight."

"Yep, love you."

"Love you too." He loved hearing Zerk say he loved him.

He set his phone aside and returned his attention to his laptop. Checking the files every now and again, but his mind was only half on his work. Zerk was screwing with his concentration. He knew they were still in the honeymoon phase and things developed quickly, friends to partners was a natural transition. *Would it always be like this?* His parents were as affectionate and in love as the night they met.

He groaned and forced his mind completely on the job at hand, or he'd never be done in time to get home to go out to dinner. Everything would work itself out, and he'd do well to remember it. Stupid doubts and what-ifs wouldn't screw up what he had with Zerk; he wouldn't let it.

17 THAT MOTHERFUCKER FUCKED UP!

What the hell was he thinking? The question played on repeat in his mind as he looked at the display of wedding rings. It wasn't like he didn't know what the hell he wanted, but why the fuck would Landon say yes? They'd only been together a matter of months.

"Zerk, are you going to look at anything or just stand there like you're getting ready to puke?" Peaches' amusement wasn't welcome.

"Why would he say yes?"

"My son loves you, Fake God knows why."

"You're so not fucking helping, why did I ask you along?" There wasn't any heat in his voice. He loved Peaches, and she'd made him feel at home since he'd met her. Having her there to help pick out rings felt right.

"Because I know his ring size and Gib is all pouting and shit about you asking me permission to marry Landon."

"He wasn't—"

"He so fucking was, men love to sulk. You know Landon would be happy with an inked ring."

He caught her stroking the ink on her ring finger.

"I know, I was going to ask for that too, but I thought he'd like something he could wear at work. Visible tattoos probably aren't always appropriate in his line of work."

"Maybe, you never know. Also, an actual ring would show all the men sniffing around my son that he's taken."

"You fucking know it." He growled at the thought of other people looking at Landon; thinking they could ask him out. Landon wouldn't cheat, but he wanted a mark everyone could see and not just the ones he put on Landon's perfect body. Those were just for the two of them.

"So possessive, never took you for the type."

"I've never been, but he's mine."

"Of that, there isn't any doubt. So, what are you thinking, simple bands for both of you?"

"Yeah, if he wears one then I should too."

"What about these?"

He looked at the ring she pointed out, it was a thick, black titanium band, simple design with no frills.

"Shouldn't it be—"

"No, it shouldn't be. This is just a symbol, nothing more and nothing less. He'll love it."

"I hope so, and I also hope he doesn't laugh in my face."

"He won't laugh, and if he does, it'll just be because he's nervous." She wrapped her arms around one of his and leaned into his side. "I always knew you'd be my first son-in-law."

"First? You have me and Landon divorced already."

"Shut up, no, I'm waiting impatiently for the rest of y'all to give me sons-in-law and grand babies."

"Oh no, me and Landon talked about this one, you're not breeding us."

"I know, I know, he's been very adamant that the rest of the guys would have to provide me with grandchildren. Although a mini Zerk would be super cute."

He groaned and called the salesperson over hoping to derail Peaches' attempt at arguing her case about them being the ones to have kids. The law degree of hers was definitely in her blood—the woman never lost an argument. He purchased two rings for Landon and himself, and he placed the box in the inner pocket of his leather jacket.

He paid and headed outside with Peaches still hugging his arm. He bumped into someone just as he turned to head back toward the shop.

"Sorry—"

Looking up his gaze collided with Ron's and all he saw was hatred.

"Hello, Ron," Peaches' voice was icy.

"Peaches, it's been awhile."

"It has been bliss."

His lips twitched at her contented sigh but hid it quickly. Although from the glare he received from Ron it hadn't been quick enough.

"Don't you work on the other side of town," he asked.

It was getting too much of a damn coincidence every time he turned around he ran into Ron. Add the man's visit to Landon's office a few weeks ago, and he was getting tired of it. The man was a spoiled brat. Now that one of his old toys was getting attention from someone else, he wanted to play with it again. If he hadn't started dating Landon, he knew Ron never would've started sniffing around.

"I had a lunch meeting at Vincent's, and as I was passing, I saw you through the window. Getting a little something for your husband, Peaches?"

"No."

Peaches was open and friendly, but he'd never seen her that cold to someone before. Even when she had to deal with people she didn't like, she was at least polite. He could tell her attitude was pissing Ron off.

He wasn't going to mention the rings. Ron would have it all over town before he had a chance to ask Landon.

"How about we have some coffee or dinner?"

"Not happening. Peaches, could ya give us a minute?" Peaches nodded and walked off to the next storefront. "Listen, motherfucker, stay away from Landon and me. I don't know what the fuck your game is, but you're not fucking up what I have with Landon with this stalk job of yours."

"I don't—"

He didn't give Ron another chance to lie to him.

"Knock off the shit. You're not making Landon jealous, and you're sure as fuck not getting me to have coffee or whatever the hell else you want. It was over months ago and—"

"You bought that little whore of yours a ring! He'll—"

He curled his fingers into his palms, snarled and took a step closer to Ron. "Listen, you little fucker, you're gonna turn around and walk away. I've had enough of your shit. You can say whatever you want about me, but you leave Landon out of it."

"I don't—"

"Ron." Peaches stepped between them. "You come near my son or Zerk at any point in the future, and I'll make sure you pay in every mortifying way I can devise starting with a restraining order served at your place of employment."

Horror turned Ron's features slack, and his perfectly tanned skin went ashen.

"Maybe a harassment lawsuit, which wouldn't go anywhere, but a judge would have to throw it out. Courts are full of frivolous lawsuits. So, you might think you can make my boys' lives miserable because you're a spoiled bitch, although, I can guarantee you don't want to fuck with me. I have plenty of resources, and not all of them are of the legal variety, do we understand each other?"

He stood back and watched Peaches with a wary expression, he'd never seen that level of anger in her eyes before. Yeah, he'd seen her pissed a few times. No, this wasn't Peaches, what disturbed him most was the cold, almost professional expression as her hazel eyes blazed. He turned a quick glance at Ron to find the man's cheeks pink, and he visibly swallowed as he took a few steps backward. Ron started to open his mouth.

"Unless it's an apology and promise to keep your narrow ass away, I'd keep those lips closed," Peaches warned.

She stepped to the side and hugged his arm again, her beautiful smile back in place.

"Why are you still here?"

Ron couldn't get away fast enough, and Zerk watched him until he disappeared at the end of the block.

"Illegal activities?"

She didn't say a word until he steered them toward the shop.

"I spent several years as a public defender before I quit to work with Gib, I made a few friends over that time. Some still owe me a few favors."

"You are truly terrifying."

"I fell in love with a heavily tattooed biker tattoo artist from the wrong side of the tracks and was disowned by family and friends. Then I raised an openly gay son in a community that's sometimes intolerant. I learned sweet only gets you so far before you gotta cut someone off at the knees."

"Vicious."

"You fucking know it."

"How did Gib propose?"

"We'd been together about two years. One morning I woke up and he was watching me sleep, which was weird because I normally had to wake him up. Our schedules were a bit backward. He said he'd gotten me something and handed me this tiny bag. When I opened it, inside was this beautiful ring, he just looked at me and raised his brows. I told him, fucking finally."

"He didn't get down on one knee after a romantic dinner?"

"Who needs all the clichéd trappings when the man you love gazes at you like you're everything he's always wanted. From minute one of meeting him, that's what it felt like. I was his everything. A ring was just a symbol of it. Something to show the world I was his. I would still be living in sin with that man even without the ring or ceremony performed by a justice of the peace."

She laid her head against his bicep, and they walked in silence back to the shop. When they arrived, Gib's weathered face brightened with a smile, and he opened his arms for his wife. She left his side and made her way to Gib taking her usual seat on his lap. He wondered if that would be him and Landon in thirty years still as in love. If he were lucky, it would be, and he dropped his head to hide his smile.

He patted the ring box, then removed his jacket and hung it up. He had to have a plan. The proposal had to be perfect. He wasn't going to fuck this up.

18 WHAT THE FUCK IS ZERK DOING?

This experience would fucking teach him to ask his mother for help with anything. He was about to rip his hair out and run screaming from the house.

"You put too much cinnamon in there," Peaches screeched from his laptop.

He was on a Skype call to get just a little help with Zerk's favorite cinnamon coffee cake. He slammed his fists onto his naked hips and spun sending the apron swinging around his bare thighs.

"I put exactly the damn amount you told me too, woman," he yelled back.

"I was watching you, and for fake Jesus sake, you need to wax your ass."

"My mother is not to comment on my ass, and Zerk likes my ass as is."

Why couldn't he be normal? Have an ordinary group of family and friends, but no he'd been cursed with the crazy, and the proof was right there. He was naked except for an apron having his mother help him make his man coffee cake because Zerk said he been craving it. Great, he should commit himself now.

"Then you shouldn't have adopted my nude cooking habit and quit thinking about committing yourself. You do this every damn time we spend quality time cooking."

"I'm disconnecting."

"No, you're not, or I'll just come over, you can't ruin my famous coffee cake that my favorite loves. I won't have him getting food poisoning."

"You do know this isn't normal?"

"Fuck normal, who needs normal. If it was normal, I would've married Edward Barstow the fourth and your ass wouldn't be here because I would've killed myself to save myself the misery of faking orgasms for fifty miserable years in suburbia."

"I could've gone without knowing that."

"Then don't push your luck or I'll break out some more truth on your fuzzy ass. Doesn't Zerk get a hairball going after—"

"Hey, hey, hey, there will be no talk of rimming and you need to lay off the gay porn and hanging out with Lucky."

"He's very informative. I never—"

Landon screamed and only stopped when he heard Zerk's booming laughter coming from the door that led in from the garage.

He spun to stare at Zerk horrified. Oh, man, Zerk hadn't experienced mother/son quality time yet. It was a part of Peaches and Landon time that he kept hidden, and now the secret was out.

"Hi, Zerk, how's my favorite son? Landon's trying to poison—"

He back up until he could reach his laptop and closed the lid to disconnect the video call.

"Hi, you're home early, how was your day?" He sounded like some demented housewife.

"Not as exciting as yours," Zerk answered as the corners of his mouth twitched.

"If you even think about laughing, I will poison you, and Scary will help me hide the body."

"Wow, the love is strong with you today." Zerk moved farther into the room and tossed his pack on the kitchen table. The big man walked over and gave his mouth a quick peck, then headed for the fridge. "Is that what I think it is?"

"It's supposed to be, but I fucked it up. I don't think I put enough baking powder in it and Mom says I put too much cinnamon. You told me you were—"

"I'm sure it'll be perfect, what do ya have left?"

"Just the eggs and milk, but it probably—"

"Mix it and put it in the pan, I'm gonna jump in the shower."

"Okay." He glanced skeptically at the havoc he'd caused in his kitchen. Flour was everywhere, yolk spilled from broken eggs turning crusty around the edges where they pooled on the counter and floor. He couldn't even make a simple fucking cake.

"Baby, stop." Warm hairy arms circled him from behind. "Did I mention how sexy it was to come home to you wearing nothing but your Kiss the Cook apron?"

"No, you failed to mention that."

"Well, it was."

Zerk's soft, yet coarse beard teased the side of his neck.

"Come here," Zerk said and walked backward tugging him along.

He let out an unmanly squeak as he fell onto Zerk's lap when the big man sat down. Rough hands turned him, and he looked down into Zerk's happy face. He'd put that there. Zerk wasn't near as grumpy acting since he'd moved in.

"What," Landon asked. Zerk's expression turned a bit pensive.

"Do you want romantic dates? You know all the flowers and fancy restaurants."

"Why would I want all that when a night at Brawlers for beers is fine with me? Or my favorite pie at the diner or just cuddling you in our recliner."

"Do you love me?"

"More than anything, where's this going?"

"Listen, I love you, have for a long time, but never thought I'd be here. I just want to do everything right. Sometimes I think I'm gonna fuck up or wake up one day and you're not gonna—"

He stopped Zerk's rambling with a kiss. "Shut up, I said I'm not going anywhere. We finally got this right and stopped pretending with the friends only bullshit. So, what's really on your mind—"

Zerk leaned back and reached inside his jacket. "Well—" Zerk pulled out a black velvet box.

"What the fuck is that?" He jumped up and pointed a shaking finger at the box.

"If that look of horror is what I'm gonna get, fucking forget it."

"Shut up, what is it?"

The lid clicked open, and two simple black rings were tucked inside. *Oh fuck, what's Zerk doing?*

"I know we never talked about the whole marriage thing. It might not even be what you want now or in the future, but I want you to wear my ring both this and inked. I know I'm fucking—"

"Put it on," he practically yelled and shoved his hand in Zerk's face.

"So that means you're going to—"

"If you don't put the fucking ring on I'll do it my damn self."

"That's not exactly a yes."

"If you even dare smile you'll go back to the guest room."

"No need to be mean."

He held his breath waiting for Zerk to slide the ring onto his finger. He didn't know if he wanted the whole ceremony, but this—the ring was perfect. The cool metal settled at the base of his finger. He took the other one from the box and did the same for Zerk.

"We're having sex," he announced and none too gentle dragged Zerk from the chair.

"What about my cake?"

"I'll make it later or is the cake more—"

He laughed as he was thrown over Zerk shoulder. Herc who'd laid quietly in the corner looked up at them, rolled his eyes and put his head back down. His arms twined around Zerk's waist, slipped beneath the cotton of his shirt and palmed his belly, the hairs tickling the hollows between his fingers.

Suddenly he flew back over Zerk's shoulder and landed with several bounces on the soft mattress.

"You are insanely sexy in nothing but that damn apron." Zerk rumbled as he reached back to jerk his t-shirt over his head.

He traced every inch of Zerk with a slow and steady gaze pausing when he got to the bulge pushing at the front of his jeans. He loved every inch of Zerk, but more than that, he loved the man's laughter and his grumpiness. It was not a get down on one knee proposal, and he didn't expect one. It didn't matter because he thought it was perfect and was completely them.

There was no need for candlelight and grand gestures, Zerk loved him and one day wanted to marry him. He planted his feet on the bed and lifted until he reached beneath him to untie the apron. Landon lowered his ass back down, raised his head and removed it.

"You're so fucking beautiful." Zerk's voice filled with desire and love. The large man finished undressing and quickly covered Landon's body.

"Do you want this?"

"I want nothing else. I've already told everyone."

"What about—"

"Even your parents, Peaches came with to help. Tomorrow night there's an engagement party at Brawlers."

He placed his hands against the thick hair on Zerk's chest and pushed. Zerk rolled to his back, and he straddled his hips. He looked down at Zerk.

"Am I gonna have to put the house up for bail?"

"We gonna talk or are we gonna fuck?"

He didn't answer just leaned forward and pushed his mouth to Zerk's. Calloused hands were everywhere, sending pleasure through his body. He couldn't get close enough. That was what he wanted and fuck if it didn't suit anyone else. Zerk was everything, and he was going to prove it, make the man believe it.

19 WHAT'S AN ENGAGEMENT PARTY WITHOUT A BARFIGHT?

They'd lost track of shots, and beer bottles were piling up. Zerk was amazed that Landon had exceeded his yearly quota of fuck uttered. Lucky had pickpocketed a hand tally clicker Crave used to do head counts at the door. He laughed loudly as Lucky's eyes widen as he checked it. Scary pulled a barstool up to the table and was sitting with his back to the wall.

"We're gonna need to cut the lightweight off, shit!" Scary snorted.

Landon raised his hand slowly and started to lift his middle finger. He wrapped his arms around his man and held tight as Scary growled. He knew the massive man had a soft spot for Landon, so he wasn't worried.

"Okay, okay, with Landon and Zerk being the first to slip into unholy matrimony, I believe this deserves a toast," Lucky announced and stood while everyone around him groaned.

"Priest, control your animal." Trouble looked at Priest with glassy eyes.

Trouble wasn't much of a drinker, but he'd been putting them away most of the night. Priest rarely drank so he volunteered as the designated driver. Good thing because most of them could barely see straight.

"Oh no, I'm not claiming this one."

"You're gonna break my wee shriveled—"

"We don't need to know about your dick," Landon piped up and caused another round of loud guffaws.

"You want me to prove my—"

Priest grabbed Lucky's hands, but Zerk took in the evil glint in their resident hyper hippie's eyes.

"Fine, I wouldn't want to cause any dick envy, this night is about Zerk and Landon. So, fuck well, fuck often—"

A body flew into Lucky, and all hell broke loose as the bar erupted into a fight. Son of a bitch, Zerk surged to his feet and followed Trouble out of the booth.

Priest moved farther into the booth to sit beside Landon. He hated crowd control especially when he'd had one too many, but the capacity crowd was more than a six-person security team could handle. He hissed as his fist connected with the first man who swung on him, and after that, it was one body after another. Some fell, some caused him to stagger and all the while he heard Landon above the crowd.

"Motherfucker, I'm not bailing y'all asses out of jail."

He dared a glance over his shoulder to find Landon and Priest standing on the half-moon bench. His inattention earned him a sucker punch from a guy half his size.

"Pay attention, Zerk, so embarrassing," Landon chided.

"You're not helping, baby," he hollered to be heard.

"Sorry," Landon so didn't sound sorry.

He swore his man was laughing at him. He backed up until he was once again in front of the booth.

"Priest, handle him," he ordered.

"Oh no, I'm wondering what I'll have to pawn of Lucky's to afford his bail."

He caught sight of Scary who stood about a head above the rest of the crowd with a twink attached to his back and probably the twink's boyfriend ineffectively landing blows to Scary's stomach.

"I'll be back."

"Yes, Arnold."

"You're so not funny."

"I'm fucking hilarious," Landon snorted. "Watch Scary's right hook and don't come up in his blind spot."

"You're having way too much fun."

He almost forgot Landon's warning when he ducked a punch from Scary. It earned him a scowl as Scary shook off the tiny man on his back.

The fight seemed to go on forever before someone yelled cops and it was like no one was covered in blood and tattered clothes. It was business as usual. The Twirled Crew returned to the booth, and he noticed the Brawler Crew regrouped on the opposite side. Scary and his business partner had their heads together as a cop approached them.

He rolled his eyes as Landon's arms twined around his neck and Landon rested his chin on the top of his head.

"Scary is gonna be so cranky after this," Landon whispered.

"I think someone broke my fucking nose," Trouble whined.

"It's fine, pretty boy, it's not even bent, but let me see." Lucky stepped in front of Trouble and set his thumbs on either side of Trouble's bloody nose, then squeezed.

"Motherfucker," Trouble yelled.

"It's fine, shit, if it were broken it would give a bit more character. Too damn perfect." Lucky was muttering to himself as he moved back to stand in front of Priest shielding him from the room.

He leaned back into Landon and waited for the usual routine of them asking what happened there. Everyone would then say nothing, and the pissed off cops would stake out the bar to catch someone for a DUI.

"Have fun tonight," he asked with a smile as he felt the vibration of Landon's laughter.

"Could've done without the bar fight, but it is a bar called Brawlers."

"We could've gone somewhere romantic just the two of us and me not gotten bruised ribs and a possible black eye."

"But you're so sexy when you play bouncer." Landon's lips sucked lightly at the side of his neck. "I'll reward you for your exceptional battle technique when we get home."

Arms twined around them, and he looked to find Lucky staring at him with a gooey-eyed expression. It was way too creepy, and he tried to shake the man off, but he held on tighter than a spider monkey.

"I so want to be you two when I grow up, all in love and shit."

"You don't have weed on you, do ya?"

"Naw, I sprinkled that shit on the floor when cops got yelled. Dammit, and Mama got me the good shit this time."

They all snorted then started to groan when a grumpy cop walked their way.

"Be cool, man, be cool." Lucky sidled away to take his place back in front of Priest.

"I'm going to need to ask y'all some questions."

It was endless questioning until they could leave. They were on their way back to town; Landon was tucked under his arm and quickly on his way to sleep. He stared down at Landon's tousled hair and his relaxed features. What the fuck had he done right? He didn't know and he sure as fuck wasn't going to question it. The streetlights illuminated Landon in equal intervals until Priest turned onto their street.

Priest parked at the curb and they said their goodbyes. He led a sleepy Landon into the house and toward their bedroom. He gently stripped the man and then tucked him under the covers. Removing his clothes, he joined Landon in bed. Zerk laid on his back as he stared up at the ceiling. Landon turned and slung an arm and leg across his body.

"I love you," Landon's whispered.

The man's breath ruffled his chest hair.

"I love you too."

He barely got the reply out before he heard Landon's soft snores. Zerk smiled to himself, he traced Landon's ribs with his fingertips and down to his bare hip in slow, lazy patterns. It was more than he'd hoped for when Ron left him, and Landon offered him a place to live.

His parents were ecstatic and swore they'd come for a visit again soon. Their crew hadn't even batted a fucking lash when Landon and he made the announcement. What happened between him and Landon was natural—the way it was meant to be. No more doubts or insecurities, he turned his head and brushed a kiss to Landon's brow. He'd make sure his man never questioned his feelings and gave Landon everything he'd dreamed of for them.

Twining his fingers through Landon's, he lifted his hand, pressed a kiss to the ring finger and swore he'd put his mark there soon.

EPILOGUE: JUST CALL HIM THE TWIRLED WORLD MATCHMAKER

A year later...

Landon looked down at the inked band of black around his ring finger and stroke it with his thumb. It looked so right there, better than the actual ring, even a year later his heart still sped up at the sight of it.

He leaned heavier into Zerk's side as they curled up on the end of one of Scary's sectionals. Their usual Sunday chill day was already in full swing even Tank showed up for once.

"I'm not going to get the fucking beer," Trouble whined from his position laid out flat on the floor.

If Trouble weren't a grown ass man, he'd say his friend was having a tantrum.

"Yes, you are. You're the only one who hasn't been drinking."

"Why don't you call Priest?"

"Why are you being such a baby about this? Get your ass up, it'll take you thirty minutes, tops."

Priest wouldn't mind stopping on his way over, but Trouble was avoiding his little crush. The man worked as a cashier at Granger's Market. Weekly, the man turned Trouble down.

Trouble and him were friends forever, and Trouble couldn't hide shit from him. His best friend was exceptionally handsome, one of those guys that made other men self-conscious. The guy just needed to see what a great catch Trouble was, but that wouldn't happen if Trouble didn't keep trying.

"Fine, but if I—" Trouble huffed and curled to a sitting position.

"It'll be okay, it's a beer run, not a walk to the fucking electric chair."

He chuckled as Trouble stormed off.

"I hope you know what the fuck you're doing."

"He's getting cranky, and I've noticed he's drinking more and not dating. Something's gotta break. The guy is super cute but extremely shy."

"What the hell are you plotting?" Scary and Tank flopped down on the opposite side of the L-shaped couch.

"Trouble's been hitting on—"

"Brody, sweet kid, not really Trouble's type. That kid screams commitment. Definitely not no-strings talent."

Scary knew more than Landon thought he did. He never thought Scary paid attention to the mundane details of his friend's lives.

"Yeah, yeah, but Trouble will never know until he tries and he's giving up. It'll do him good to learn a bit of humility."

"He does get ass a little too easily. That cute, perfect smile and the dimple, they can't fall to their knees fast enough," Scary sounded disgusted.

"Jealous, Scary, not getting any," Landon asked.

Tank snorted his beer and leaned forward as he coughed and laughed. He loved the silent man to death. He assumed the scar hidden beneath Tank's beard attributed to the silence.

"That's what you get, asshole, I get more than you do."

Tank shrugged like it didn't matter and earned a hard shove that sent him sideways.

"Children, children, no need to fight over who gets the most ass." Landon checked the time. He knew Trouble would be parking any minute. If Trouble followed his usual M.O. of a pep talk before he went inside, Landon had time to torture Trouble some more.

He shifted and stretched out his legs to dig his phone out of his pocket. He scrolled through his messages to get to the conversation between Trouble and him. He typed out a quick message and hit send.

Landon: *Beer! Now! - The Guys*

"You just love to cause trouble."

"Would you prefer to be a target of my exceptional matchmaking skills?"

"Fuck you, man, the only thing permanent I want is ink, so keep your lovey-dovey happy relationship bullshit to yourself."

"Aw, someone sounds so bitter."

Scary growled, and Zerk wrapped his arm around him as he laughed. He lifted his hands to run his fingers along Zerk's hairy forearms. Tracing the muscles and veins. His phone beeped, but Zerk picked it up first.

Landon snickered as he read the reply.

Trouble: *Shut up!*

"He's so cranky, man needs someone."

"I'm sure you'll find him the perfect boyfriend. If anything, you're stubborn as fuck."

Yes, he was, and he wanted his best friend happy and Trouble hadn't been that in a long time. He was happy, and he wanted that for the rest of them too. It had nothing to do with the way Zerk made him feel, but had everything to do with knowing his friend's past, well, most of it. Trouble kept too much to himself.

"Quit worrying, Trouble will be alright."

"I know." He shifted his body and turned his head to give Zerk a kiss. "But I have a good feeling about this one."

The conversation dropped as Priest and Lucky came down the steps. Those two were something all their own. He could only work matchmaker magic one at a time. First Trouble then he'd work on the rest. He was going to find these crazy shits boyfriends if it killed them.

THE END

ABOUT THE AUTHOR

By day, J.M. is an introverted cook hiding out in her kitchen in the middle of nowhere Ohio, by night and any free time she may have, she is a writer of mainly LGBTQ Fiction and Erotica. Although. she's equal opportunity when it comes to telling a story, she'll even write a bit of straight erotic romance when the mood strikes.

She has been writing for years in old notebooks. At the age of eight, she wrote the worst poem in the history of poetry, but it sparked her love for writing. She reads too much and loves to get lost in other worlds and her favorite stories have to include laughter and having the reader doing at least one double take. Thirty-something, forever restless she uses her stories to ground herself, and find her place of peace.

WHERE TO FIND J.M.
www.jmdabneyauthor.com

AVAILABLE NOW

TROUBLE
Twirled World Ink 2

Welcome to Twirled World Ink where the crazies run the asylum.

Model perfect Jimmy "Trouble" Carver had never heard the word no. Tattooed, sexy and the quintessential bad boy, Trouble had men falling over themselves to get to him. What people didn't know about him was he was self-conscious even if life was easy for him. He'd started out as an apprentice at Twirled World Ink after college and never looked back. Trouble was exactly where he wanted to be, although there was one speed bump, his crush refused to go out on a date.

Brody Vaughn worked in a dead-end job, barely making it from paycheck to paycheck. He didn't have much time for anyone other than his five-year-old daughter Mina, and besides, he'd never quite found a place in this world he fit. Chunky and average, that's how he felt, except for when Trouble came into the grocery store where he worked. The flirty, gorgeous man asked him out every week with a sexy smile, but Brody had to refuse. It wasn't as if he wanted to say no, it was just the fact that how could he date a man he knew he had no business trying to keep.

The Crazies of Twirled World Ink excel at one thing, matchmaking, and they are determined their resident bad boy would get his man. They just had to make sure that neither Trouble or Brody screwed up their plan.

✦ ✦ ✦

1 HE SHOULD'VE ESCAPED WHILE HE HAD THE CHANCE

We don't need beer this bad! Jimmy "Trouble" Carver gripped the steering wheel until his knuckles turned white and stared at the entrance of Granger Grocery. His friends hated him. He'd asked the cashier out on a date almost weekly for the past year, and each time, Brody turned him down.

His phone beeped beside him, he reached for it and checked the message. It was from his best friend, Landon.

Landon: *Beer! Now! - The Guys*

Why the fuck did he stay sober? If he'd drank a few beers, they wouldn't have asked him to deal with yet another humiliation. Everyone claimed he had it too easy when it came to finding a hookup. He wouldn't deny it, apart from his looks, he didn't have many redeeming qualities.

He angrily typed out a response.

Trouble: *Shut up!*

He sent the reply, shifted his hips and shoved his phone into his back pocket. They had no sympathy. What the fuck was he doing here? Because they refused to head to the store themselves. He huffed and got out then jogged toward the store. If he were lucky, Brody wouldn't be working. He slowed and walked through the automatic doors. His gaze was drawn toward the checkout lanes. Trouble nearly tripped over his feet when he saw Brody standing at his usual post at register two. Unfortunately, it seemed Brody drew the short straw today to work the afternoon lull alone.

He grabbed a cart and headed straight for the beer aisle. Picked up several twelve packs of beer, then spun toward snacks and stocked up. He slowed down and turned his cart into lane two.

"Hi, Trouble."

"Brody, how you doing?"

He unloaded the items onto the belt. Trouble barely looked at Brody. He knew what the cutie looked like. Trouble studied Brody enough to describe him in detail. Brody was short, slightly chunky and cute as fuck. Not his usual type, but the first time he'd noticed Brody he'd been helpless to resist asking him out. Only the first of many polite declines. He didn't know what Brody had against him because he'd caught the other man watching him.

"Only a few more minutes left on my shift." Each word was punctuated by a beep as Brody slid items over the scanner. "Party planning?"

"We're all at Scary's for a movie night. It's a standing tradition."

"Sounds like fun."

There seemed to be a bit of wistfulness in Brody's tone. Trouble almost opened his mouth to ask the man to join them. He couldn't take another rejection.

"We all went on our early morning ride."

Conversation wasn't exactly Trouble's strong suit and that time didn't seem to improve his skills.

Brody nodded and gave him the total. He pulled out the cash they'd pooled before he'd left.

"Daddy, Daddy," a squeaky little voice had his head popping up to see a chunky little girl with lopsided pigtails bounce up to Brody and wrap her arms around Brody's thigh.

"Honey, I told you to wait for me in the office. We're almost ready." Brody looked at him. "Sorry." The man's tanned face turned a bit pink.

"That's okay. Hi, I'm Trouble." He gave her a small wave, and the little girl hid her face against Brody's leg. She was a perfect mini-version of Brody.

"Is he in trouble, Daddy?"

The question made him bark out a loud laugh, and the color on Brody's cheeks brightened. It made Brody incredibly adorable, and Trouble wanted the man more. Trouble hadn't thought it possible.

"No, that's his name, like when I call you honey, it's a name friends and family call you."

He had to admit the two of them were the cutest duo he'd ever seen.

"Oh, hi, Trouble. I'm Mina."

"Very nice to meet you, Mina."

"My babysitter had an emergency."

Brody seemed to get more embarrassed by the second. He didn't understand why though. Trouble wondered where Mina's mom was. His gaze fell to the bare ring finger, but that didn't prove anything.

"Why don't the two of you—"

"We already have plans."

Hurt tightened his chest, and Trouble wanted to escape as quick as possible.

"Okay. I better get going before the boys start texting me again." He held out his hand for his change, hauled his purchases into his cart and ran as fast as he could without being too obvious.

You're such a fucking loser, Trouble, he muttered to himself. All he wanted to do was drive straight to his place, but since he lived with two of his friends, he would just set himself up for an extra brutal ribbing later.

♦ ♦ ♦

Three a.m. found him staring at the ceiling of Scary's living room. Landon's back to him a few feet away as his friend curled up with his partner Berserker. Lucky had his head resting on Priest's stomach as they softly snored. Scary was in his room.

Sunday nights they all crashed at Scary's even if they didn't have too much to drink; it was an unspoken rule no one drove home. He'd tried to sneak out, but Landon ambushed him and dragged Trouble back inside the house.

"You're thinking too loud," Landon whined in a sleepy voice.

"I just can't—"

In usual Landon fashion, he interrupted someone when he didn't want to wait to listen to their bullshit. "You've got to get over it."

Not everything was as easy as Landon wanted to make it. Over the past year, Landon subjected him to countless speeches.

"There's nothing to—"

"Move on."

"Quit interrupting—"

"Quit sounding like my boyfriend."

"Then shut up and let someone finish a fucking thought."

"Not if their opinion is stupid." Landon turned over and cuddled up to his side.

"Your man won't like you cuddling with other people."

"Yeah right."

To prove his point, Zerk turned over laying his arm across both of them. He shook his head, Landon giggled as Zerk's massive, hairy arm cuddled them both.

"Did you try asking him out again?"

He didn't want to talk about it, yet knew Landon wouldn't let it go. When his best friend fixated on something, Landon would see it through until the end or until someone threatened him with death.

"I invited him and his daughter to hang out, he turned me down before I finished asking."

"Daughter?"

"Yeah, cutest thing I've ever seen." He smiled in the dark. "This beautiful long curly hair and huge blue eyes. Mina was like this cute, tiny female version of Brody."

"So, you think he's straight," Landon asked.

He hated to think so because he didn't mistake the glances Brody sometimes gave him. "Probably, if I'm lucky he's bi."

"Still determined to get Brody to go out with you?"

"Maybe. I keep saying it's the last time, but I just keep setting myself up for rejection." No one could say Trouble was all that smart. They'd skipped over him when it came to brains but heaped good looks on him.

"Trouble, you've never been told no. You bat those lovely lashes, and everyone falls over themselves to do your bidding. I think it's good for you not to get your way."

"You're all heart," Trouble huffed.

"I don't think you're as pretty as you think you are."

"That's because you like grizzly bears masquerading as men."

"My man is sexy in all his hairy, husky glory."

"Whatever you say, he's not my type."

"Cute, cuddly single Daddies your type, huh?"

Trouble sighed and lifted his hands to cover his face. He didn't want to admit he hadn't had a date since Brody started turning him down. Like he didn't get enough shit from his friends already. Admitting Brody decimated his ego would be like bleeding out in a tank full of sharks. Also, no matter how hard he tried, he couldn't get Brody out of his head.

He slipped his arm between Zerk and Landon settling the smaller man's head on his shoulder.

"I'm getting too old for this shit."

"Are we having a quarter life crisis? Didn't we just celebrate your thirtieth birthday?"

Landon petted Trouble's bare chest like it was a regular occurrence. It was, none of them understood personal space. Last time they went out in a group they kept getting asked who was dating whom.

"I think I'm losing my looks."

Landon's hysterical laughter started out loud enough to wake the neighborhood before Landon slammed his hand over his mouth to stifle it.

"What's so fucking funny?"

"Jimmy *Trouble* Carver, I've known you for years, and I think you just get prettier every year. Come on, you're the tattooed, pierced, sexy bad boy that makes jockstraps fall in his wake. One man tells you no, and you go all emo like some teen goth girl who's run out of black eyeliner."

"Um, did you just compliment and insult me in the same breath?"

"Yes, maybe your cute boy has a partner at home? Probably how he got the kid."

"Brody's never—"

"Some heavily pierced and tattooed heathen called Trouble hits on you, what would a responsible—"

"Hey, I'm responsible."

"Yes, you are."

The petting resumed, and he closed his eyes. Landon was telling him what he wanted to hear to shut him up.

"You've gotta stop stressing about it."

That was easier said than done. "You're right."

"Now, keep those blue eyes closed and get some sleep. I'm frightened for your clients today."

"You're so funny, Pipsqueak."

"I know."

Trouble didn't reply and pretended to sleep. Trouble was stupid; he knew it, and his friends did too. That didn't mean the rejection didn't hurt especially when, for the first time in his life, he cared when someone said no. If someone didn't want to go out with him, he shrugged it off and moved on. He shifted to get more comfortable and cuddled Landon tighter. It was sad the closest thing to intimacy he had in close to a year was a platonic cuddle from two of his best friends. When had Trouble Carver fallen so far?